I SURVIVED

COLLECTION

by **Lauren Tarshis**

illustrated by **Scott Dawson**

Scholastic Inc.

Text pages 1–204 copyright © 2010 by Lauren Tarshis
Illustrations pages 1–204 copyright © 2010 by Scholastic Inc.
Text pages 205–415 copyright © 2011 by Lauren Tarshis
Illustrations pages 205–415 copyright © 2011 by Scholastic Inc.

ISBN 978-1-338-10249-9

10 9 8 7 6 5 4 3 2 1   16 17 18 19 20

Printed in the U.S.A. 40
First printing 2016
Designed by Yaffa Jaskoll
Series design by Tim Hall

TABLE OF CONTENTS

THE NEW YORK TIMES BESTSELLING SERIES
I SURVIVED
THE SINKING OF
THE TITANIC, 1912
by Lauren
Tarshis
SCHOLASTIC

I SURVIVED

THE SINKING OF THE *TITANIC*, 1912

by Lauren Tarshis

illustrated by Scott Dawson

Scholastic Inc.

I SURVIVED

THE SINKING OF THE *TITANIC*, 1912

by Lauren Tarshis

illustrated by Scott Dawson

Scholastic Inc.

CHAPTER 1

MONDAY, APRIL 15, 1912

2:00 A.M.

ON THE DECK OF RMS *TITANIC*

The *Titanic* was sinking.

The gigantic ship had hit an iceberg.

Land was far, far away.

Ten-year-old George Calder stood on the deck.

He shivered because the night was freezing cold.

And because he was scared. More scared than he'd ever been before.

More scared than when Papa swore he'd send George to the army school, far from everything and everyone.

More scared, even, than the time the black panther chased him through the woods back home in Millerstown, New York.

The deck of the *Titanic* was packed with people. Some were running and shouting.

"Help us!"

"Take my baby!"

"Jump!"

Some just plain screamed. Children cried. A gunshot exploded across the deck. But George didn't move.

Just hold on, he told himself, gripping the rail. Like maybe he could hold up the ship.

He couldn't look down at that black water. He kept his eyes on the sky. He had never seen so many stars. Papa said that Mama watched over him from heaven.

Could Mama see him now?

The ship lurched.

"We're going down!" a man shouted.

George closed his eyes, praying this was all a dream.

Even more terrible sounds filled the air. Glass shattering. Furniture crashing. More screams and cries. A bellowing sound, like a giant beast was dying a terrible death. George tried to hold the rail. But he lost his grip. He tumbled, smashing his head on the deck.

And then George couldn't see anything.

Even the stars above him seemed to go black.

CHAPTER 2

19 HOURS EARLIER . . .

SUNDAY, APRIL 14, 1912

7:15 A.M.

FIRST CLASS SUITE, B DECK, RMS *TITANIC*

George woke up early that morning, half expecting to hear Papa calling him for chores.

But then he remembered: the *Titanic*!

He was on the greatest ship in the world.

It was their fifth day at sea. George and his

eight-year-old sister, Phoebe, had spent two months in England with their aunt Daisy. What a time they had! As a surprise for George's tenth birthday, Aunt Daisy took them to see the Tower of London, where they used to chop off your head if the king didn't like you.

Now they were heading back to America.

Back to Papa and their little farm in upstate New York.

George got out of bed and knelt by the small, round window that looked out on the ocean.

"Morning," said Phoebe, peering through the silk curtains of her bed and fumbling for her spectacles. Her curly brown hair was practically standing straight up. "What were you looking for?"

George had to smile. Phoebe always had a question, even at the crack of dawn.

Maybe that's why she was the smartest little sister in the world.

"I thought I saw a giant squid," George said. "And it's coming to get us!"

George rushed over and grabbed Phoebe with wiggly squid arms. She curled up into a ball and laughed.

She was still laughing when Aunt Daisy came in. Even in her robe and slippers, Aunt Daisy was the prettiest lady on the whole ship. Sometimes George couldn't believe she was so old: twenty-two!

"What's this?" Aunt Daisy said. "You know the rule: No having fun without me!"

Phoebe sat up and put her arms around George. "Georgie said he saw a giant squid."

Aunt Daisy laughed. "I wouldn't doubt it. Everyone wants to get a look at the *Titanic*. Even sea monsters."

George halfway believed it. He'd never imagined anything like the *Titanic*.

Aunt Daisy called the ship a floating palace. But it was way better than the cold and dusty castles they'd seen in England. They had three whole rooms—one for Phoebe and George, one for Aunt Daisy, and one for sitting around and doing nothing. They even had a man, a steward named Henry. He had bright red hair and an Irish accent that made everything he said sound like a jolly song.

"Some fresh towels for your bath?" he would say. "Some cocoa before bed?"

And just before they turned out the lights for the night, Henry would knock on their door and peep his head in.

"Is there anything else you might need?" he'd ask.

George kept trying to think of *something* he needed.

But what could you ever need on the *Titanic*?

The ship had everything, even a swimming pool with ocean water heated up like a bath, even gold silk curtains for your bed so you could pretend you were sleeping in a pirate's den, even three dining rooms where you could eat anything you wanted. Last night George had eaten two plates of roast beef, veal and ham pie, carrots sweet as candy, and a mysterious dessert called meringue pudding. It tasted like sugary clouds.

Actually, there *was* one thing missing from the *Titanic*: the New York Giants baseball team. George wondered what Henry would say if George said, "I need shortstop Artie Fletcher right away!"

Probably Henry would say, "Coming right up, sir!"

George grinned just thinking about it.

But Aunt Daisy wasn't smiling at him. She looked very serious.

"We have to make the most of our last three days at sea," Aunt Daisy said in a low voice. "I want you to promise me, George. *No more* trouble!"

George gulped.

Was she really still mad at him for last night?

He'd slid down the banister of the grand staircase in the first class lobby. How could he

resist? The wood was so shiny and polished, curving around like a ride at the fair.

"That lady could have moved out of the way," George said.

"How could she?" Phoebe said. "She was wearing a hundred pounds of diamonds!"

Aunt Daisy almost smiled. George could tell.

No, she could never stay mad at George for long.

Aunt Daisy put her face very close to George's. She had freckles on her nose, just like George and Phoebe.

"No more trouble," she repeated, tapping his chest. "I don't want to have to send a telegram to your father."

George's stomach tightened into a baseball.

"Don't tell Papa!" Phoebe said. "He'll send George away to that army school!"

"I'll be good," George promised. "I will, really."

"You better be," Aunt Daisy said.

CHAPTER 3

George didn't mean to get into trouble.

It's just that he got these *great* ideas.

Like on their first day at sea, when he had climbed up the huge ladder into the crow's nest.

"Aunt Daisy!" he'd yelled, waving his arms.

She had looked up. And she'd almost fainted.

And yesterday George had explored the entire ship. Aunt Daisy kept warning him that he'd get lost. She said the ship was like a maze. But George could always find his way. Even in the huge forest that stretched out behind their farm. Mama used to say that George had a map of the world behind his eyes.

He saw the engine rooms and the boiler rooms, and wound up on the third-class recreation deck. He was watching some boys play marbles when he noticed that he wasn't alone. A little boy was staring up at him with huge eyes the color of amber glass.

"See," the boy said. "See."

And he held out a postcard of the Statue of Liberty. He looked so proud, like he'd carved that big lady himself. George felt like he had to show something in return, so he took out his good-luck charm, the bowie knife Papa had given him for his ninth birthday. He let the little boy run his fingers across the handle, which was carved from an elk's antler.

"Enzo," the little boy said, puffing out his chest and pointing to himself.

"George," said George.

"Giorgio!" the little boy cried with a smile.

A man sitting near them laughed. He was reading an Italian-English dictionary and had the same huge eyes as the boy. George guessed right that he was Enzo's father.

"Marco," he said, shaking George's hand. "You are our first American friend."

Marco must have been studying that dictionary pretty hard, because George understood everything he said. George learned that Enzo was four years old. He'd lost his mama too. He and Marco came from a little town in Italy, and now they were moving to New York City. George told Marco about their farm and their trip and explained that any decent person living in New York had to be a Giants fan. For some reason, Marco thought that was funny.

When it was time for George to leave, Enzo got upset. Very upset.

"Giorgio!" he howled, loud enough for the entire ship to hear.

17

People stared and put their hands over their ears. Marco promised that they'd see George again, but Enzo wouldn't quit howling. George had never heard anything so loud.

By the time Enzo let go of George's leg and George ran back up to the suite, Aunt Daisy was practically howling too.

"I thought you fell overboard!" she cried.

But even then she wasn't really mad.

She didn't get *really* mad until last night.

How that lady screamed when George came sliding down the banister — like he really was a giant squid.

George didn't mind getting yelled at. He was used to it. Not a day at school went by without Mr. Landers shouting "George! Settle down!" And Papa, well, he always seemed to be mad at George.

But not Aunt Daisy. And being on this trip was supposed to make her happy, happy for the first time since her husband died last year. It had been Uncle Cliff's dream to be on the maiden voyage of the *Titanic*. He'd struck it rich selling automobiles and had plenty of money to pay for one of the biggest suites on the ship.

When Uncle Cliff had his accident, George was sure Aunt Daisy would cancel the trip. Instead she'd invited George and Phoebe to go with her.

And to George's shock, Papa said they could.

"Your aunt's going on this trip to find a little peace," he'd said to George. "I expect you to be a perfect gentleman."

And if he wasn't, George knew he'd be shipped off to that army school for sure. Papa had been talking about that place ever since George had brought the two-foot rat snake to school to show Mr. Landers — because they were studying reptiles!

George had been perfect the whole time in England. He'd let Aunt Daisy drag him to a fancy clothes store for a new pair of boots. He even learned to drink tea without spitting it back into the cup.

But, well, the *Titanic*.

The ship gave him so many great ideas!

But now he'd really be perfect.

No more ideas for the rest of the voyage.

CHAPTER 4

Phoebe wasn't taking any chances with George.

"I'm not letting you out of my sight," she announced after they'd finished breakfast. "I'm your guardian angel."

"I didn't know angels wore spectacles," he said, tugging on one of Phoebe's curls.

"The smart ones do," Phoebe said, grabbing George's arm. She offered him a lemon drop from the little silver tin she'd been carrying around since London.

George made a face. He hated those old-lady candies.

George wanted to go find Marco and Enzo and hear more about Italy. He wanted to ride the elevators up and down. Hardly any other ship in the world had elevators! Better yet, he wanted to find Mr. Andrews, the ship's designer.

When Mr. Andrews had stopped by their table at dinner the first night, George thought he was just another boring millionaire coming over to kiss Aunt Daisy's hand.

But Mr. Andrews was different.

"You *built* the *Titanic*?" said George.

Mr. Andrews smiled. "Not by myself. It took thousands of men to build her. But I did design her, that's true."

He invited George and Phoebe to come with him to the first class writing room. He unrolled the ship's blueprints across a long, polished table.

It was like looking at the skeleton of a giant beast.

"She's the biggest moving object ever built," Mr. Andrews explained. "Eleven stories tall. Forty-five thousand tons of steel. And longer than four city blocks."

"Our aunt says nothing bad can happen to this ship," Phoebe said. "People say it's unsinkable."

"No ship is safer," Mr. Andrews said. "That is certainly true."

"What if the *Titanic* was hit by a meteor?" said Phoebe, whose latest obsession was outer space. She was determined to see a shooting star before they docked in New York.

Mr. Andrews didn't laugh or roll his eyes like Mr. Landers did when Phoebe asked her questions.

"I hadn't planned on any meteors hitting the ship," Mr. Andrews said thoughtfully. "But I'd like to think she could take almost anything and still float."

Phoebe seemed satisfied.

"Are there any secret passages?" said George.

Mr. Andrews studied his blueprints, and then pointed to the boiler rooms.

"There are escape ladders," he said. "They run up the starboard side of the ship, up two decks, through the stokers' quarters, and into their dining hall. I hear the crew likes using them instead of the stairs."

George could have stayed there all night. He

asked a million questions and Mr. Andrews answered every single one.

"I was like you when I was a boy," Mr. Andrews said just before Aunt Daisy came to haul George off to bed. "One day I predict you'll build a ship of your own."

George knew that would never happen. He could barely get through a day at school. But he liked that Mr. Andrews said it. And he sure wanted to find those secret ladders.

But Phoebe had different ideas.

First she dragged George to the first class library so she could check out a book on Halley's comet. Then she took him on a walk on the boat deck. He felt like a dog.

"Strange," Phoebe said, looking at the lifeboats that hung just off the deck. "There are only sixteen boats. That's not nearly enough for everyone."

"The ship's unsinkable," George said. "So do we really need lifeboats at all?"

Phoebe stared at the boats and shrugged. "I guess you're right," she said. And then she announced that it was time to see how many ladies were wearing hats with blue feathers.

George groaned.

This would be the most boring day of his life.

But at least nobody was yelling at him.

CHAPTER 5

At dinner that night, Aunt Daisy raised her glass. "To George! No trouble for one entire day!"

They clinked their glasses together just as an old man stopped by their table.

"Mrs. Key," the man said to Aunt Daisy. "I've been meaning to say hello."

"Mr. Stead!" Aunt Daisy said. "What a pleasure. This is George, my nephew, and Phoebe, my niece."

Mr. Stead nodded hello.

"So," Aunt Daisy said. "What brings you onto this magnificent ship?"

"Oh, I couldn't miss it," he said. "I think all of society is on this ship. I hear there's even an Egyptian princess on board."

"Really!" Aunt Daisy said. "I haven't met her!"

"Well, none of us have. She's traveling in the first class baggage room."

"Excuse me?" Aunt Daisy said.

"The princess is more than twenty-five hundred years old," Mr. Stead said.

George's ears perked up.

"I'm not sure I understand," Aunt Daisy said.

"She's a mummy," Mr. Stead said.

"A mummy!" Phoebe gasped.

"That's right," Mr. Stead said. "From a tomb near Thebes. I understand she belongs to a man named Mr. Burrows. People are saying he sold the coffin to the British Museum. Then he packed the princess herself in a wooden crate. Apparently he's bringing her back for his collection. Some say it's bad luck to take a mummy from its tomb."

"I'm glad I'm not the superstitious type!" Aunt Daisy said.

Mr. Stead chuckled. "In any case, nothing can harm this ship. Not even the curse of a mummy!"

Mr. Stead tipped his hat and said good-bye.

"Mr. Stead is a very famous writer in England," Aunt Daisy said. "You never know who you'll meet on the *Titanic*!"

And then it hit George, the best idea ever.

That mummy! He had to see it.

Maybe this day wasn't so boring after all.

CHAPTER 6

George didn't tell Phoebe or Aunt Daisy about his plan.

He figured he'd head down to the first class baggage room after they went to sleep. He'd find Mr. Burrows's crate, pry it open, and take a quick peek at the mummy. He'd be back in bed and snoring away before anyone knew he was gone.

It was almost eleven-fifteen when Phoebe was

finally asleep and the light was out under Aunt Daisy's door. George crept out of bed. He quickly got dressed and put his knife in his pocket. He'd need it for prying off the lid of the crate. And who knew? Maybe there was a live cobra in the box too. George could hope, couldn't he?

George opened the door and peeked into the hallway. He wanted to avoid Henry, who seemed to have eyes in the back of his bright orange head. He wouldn't like George creeping around so late at night.

But the hallway was quiet. There was no noise at all except for the quiet hum of the engines, rising up from the bottom of the ship. George loved that noise. It made him think of crickets in the woods at night.

In fact, being out here all by himself reminded him of the nights at home when he sneaked out into the woods while Papa and Phoebe were asleep.

He'd head out when his mind was filled with restless thoughts.

About why Papa was always mad at him, or why he didn't try harder in school.

And of course Mama.

Almost three years had passed since she died. George tried not to think about her too much. But some nights when he closed his eyes, he'd remember her smile. Or her smell when she hugged him close. Like fresh grass and sweet flowers.

And that song she'd sing to wake George up in the morning:

"Awake, awake.
It's now daybreak!
But don't forget your dreams. . . ."

Thinking about Mama was like standing close to a fire. Warm at first. But get too close and it hurt too much.

Much better to stay clear of those thoughts.

Nothing cleared George's mind quicker than being in the woods. He never stayed out for more than an hour or two. . . . Except for that night back in October.

George was heading back toward home when he heard a terrible sound, like a little girl screaming. He turned around, and in the dark distance he saw two glowing yellow eyes.

Some old-timers said there were black panthers in the woods, but George never believed it.

But as the yellow eyes got closer, George could see the outline of a huge cat, with two glistening fangs.

George told himself not to run. He knew he'd never outrun the panther.

But he couldn't help it—he ran as fast as he could. Branches cut his face, but he didn't slow down.

Any second the panther would leap up and tackle George. Its claws would tear him apart.

George could feel the cat right behind him; he could smell its breath, like rotting meat. George grabbed a fallen branch. He turned and waved it in front of him. The panther lunged and grabbed the branch in its jaws.

George let go of the stick and scrambled up a tree, climbing as high as he could go.

The cat dropped the branch and came after him, like a shadow with glowing eyes.

George pulled out his knife.

He waited until the cat's front paws were on the small branch just below him. And then, with all his might, he chopped at the branch with his knife.

Crack.

The branch broke free.

The giant cat tumbled through the air, screaming and crashing through the branches, and then hit the ground with a thud.

There was silence.

And then the cat stood up. It looked up at George for a long moment.

And it turned and walked slowly back into the woods.

George stayed in the tree until it was just about light, and made it into bed just before Papa woke up.

His friends at school refused to believe George when he told them, even when he swore on his heart.

"No way."

"Big fat lie."

"Next thing you'll be saying is that you've been signed by the Giants." Their laughter rose up around George, but it didn't bother him, because right then he realized that it didn't matter what they thought.

George knew he'd faced down the panther.

And he'd never forget it.

CHAPTER 7

Just thinking about seeing the mummy made George happy. He went down five flights of stairs to G deck and practically skipped along the long hallway toward the front of the ship. He ducked into doorways a few times to hide from the night stewards. But he had no trouble finding his way, not like Phoebe, who got lost walking from the dining room to the washroom.

"Next time I'll leave a trail of bread crumbs,

like Hansel and Gretel," she'd said, their first day on board.

"How about lemon drops?" George had suggested.

Phoebe had giggled.

The hold was in the very front of the ship, past the mail sorting room and the cabins where the stokers and firemen stayed. Too bad, George thought, that there wasn't time to sneak in and see the escape ladders. Luckily there were two more days at sea.

George walked right through the doors of the first class baggage room and down a steep metal staircase that led to the hold. All around him were crates and trunks and bags neatly stacked on shelves and lined up on the floor.

It took him a minute to figure out that everything was arranged in alphabetical order, by the owners' names, and a few minutes to find the *B*s.

And there it was, a plain wooden crate stamped with the words:

MR. DAVID BURROWS
NEW YORK CITY
CONTENTS FRAGILE

George smiled to himself.

This was going to be easy.

He took out his knife and started to pry off the lid. He worked carefully, prying each nail loose so he'd be able to close the crate tight again when he was finished.

He'd made it halfway around when he heard a strange sound.

The hair on his arms prickled.

It was the same feeling he'd had the night of the panther, that someone — or something — was watching him.

George stared at the crate, his heart pounding.

And before he could even take a breath,
something leaped out of the shadows and pushed
him to the ground.

George looked up, half expecting to see a
mummy rising out of the crate, her arms reaching
for George's throat.

What he saw was almost as horrifying.

It was a man with glittering blue eyes and a scar running down the side of his face.

He grabbed George's knife out of his hand. The man was small, but very strong.

"I'll take this," he said, admiring it. Then he looked George up and down.

"So," the man said. "Trying to fill your pockets with some first class loot?"

George realized he must be a robber. George had caught him in the act!

"Uh, no, I'm . . ."

The man pointed to George's boots. "Which trunk did you steal those from? Cost more than a third class ticket, I'd say."

George shook his head. "I got them in London," he said, and too late realized he'd made a mistake.

"Ah, a prince from first class," the man said with a hearty laugh. "Just down here for a little thrill? What's your name?"

"George," said George softly.

"Prince George," the man said, bowing in a joking way. "A pity those boots wouldn't fit me," he added, standing up. "But you do have something I'd like. Your key. Always wanted to see one of those first class cabins."

There was no way George could let this man up to the suite! He'd jump overboard before he let him near Aunt Daisy and Phoebe.

"There's a mummy down here!" he blurted out. "It's worth millions! It's in that crate!"

The man raised an eyebrow.

George kept talking.

"I thought I could sneak it off the ship and sell it in New York," George lied. "My father's business is bad. I thought if I could sell it . . ."

The man looked at the crate.

"I like the way you think," he said.

He waved the knife at George and told him not to move. And then he quickly worked the knife around the lid. Obviously he'd done this many times before.

He lifted the lid off the crate. But before either of them could look inside, there was a tremendous rumbling noise, and the entire hold began to shake so hard that George almost fell. The shaking got stronger and stronger, the noise louder and louder, like thunder exploding all around them. A trunk tumbled off a shelf and hit the scar-faced man on the head. The knife clattered to the floor, but George didn't try to get it. Here was his chance to escape. He spun around, ran up the stairs, and darted out the door.

CHAPTER 8

George ran as fast as he could down the hall. He heard shouting behind him, but he didn't stop until he was back on B deck, safe again in first class.

A steward hurried past him with a stack of clean towels.

"Good evening, sir," he said.

George nodded, out of breath.

Nothing could happen to him up here, he knew. So why was his heart still pounding?

It was the ship, he realized — that thundering noise. That shaking in the hold. Had a boiler exploded? Had a steam pipe burst?

An eerie silence surrounded him, and George's heart skipped a beat as he realized that the engines had been turned off. The quiet rumbling had stopped.

Just outside, George heard people talking loudly. Did they know what was happening?

George went out onto the deck and walked over to the small crowd of men. Most were still dressed in their dinner tuxedos and puffing on cigars. They were standing at the rail, pointing and laughing at something happening on the well deck, one level below. What was so funny?

George squeezed between two men and looked over the rail.

At first he was sure his eyes were playing tricks. It looked like the well deck had been through a winter storm. It was covered with ice and slush. A bunch of young men in tattered coats and hats were pelting each other with balls of ice, roaring with laughter like kids having a snowball fight.

"What's happened?" asked a man who'd walked up behind George.

"The ship nudged an iceberg!" said an old man with a bushy mustache. He didn't sound worried.

An iceberg!

"Is that why they've stopped the engines?" said the new man. "Because of some ice on the deck?"

"Just being cautious, it seems, following regulations," said the older fellow. "I spoke to one of the officers. He assured me we'll be underway any moment. Hey there!" he yelled down to the young men below. "Toss some of that ice up here!"

One of the gang picked up a piece of ice the size of a baseball. He threw it, but the man with the bushy mustache missed. George reached out and made a clean catch with one hand. The crowd cheered. George held up the ice and smiled. Then he held it out to the man.

"Keep it, son!" he said. "There's plenty for everyone."

The piece of ice was heavier than George had expected.

He sniffed it and wrinkled his nose.

It smelled like old sardines!

More ice balls came sailing up from below, and the men jostled to catch them.

Their laughter and cheers rose up around George, and the fear he'd felt in the baggage hold faded away. From up here, on the deck of this incredible ship, George felt powerful. Nothing could hurt him on the *Titanic*.

Not a meteor falling from space. Not a giant squid.

Not the scar-faced man.

George squinted out into the distance, hoping to see the iceberg, but the sea faded into darkness.

His teeth were chattering now. It was so much

colder than it had been at dinnertime. He wanted to be back in bed, curled up under his fancy first class sheets and blankets.

The corridor was still quiet as George crept toward his suite.

As he was letting himself in, he stepped on something that made a crunching sound under his boot. At first George thought that it was ice or a piece of glass. But when he picked up his heel, he saw that the carpet was covered with yellow crystals.

George smiled. It was just one of Phoebe's lemon drops.

George let himself in, easing the door shut.

Phoebe's bed curtains were closed. The light under Aunt Daisy's door was off.

George quickly changed into his pajamas and climbed into bed.

Yes, he was safe, he told himself.

He tried to go to sleep, but as the minutes ticked by, his mind got restless.

It hit him that his knife was gone, forever, and the total silence of the ship seemed to press down on him. Why hadn't the engines started up again?

He lay wide awake, listening and wondering.

It was almost a relief when he heard someone knocking on their door.

CHAPTER 9

It was Henry.

"Hello, George," said Henry. "Can I speak to Mrs. Key, please?"

Henry wore his usual polite smile, but his voice wasn't jolly.

"What is it?" said Aunt Daisy, stepping out of her room.

"So sorry to barge in like this, ma'am," Henry said. "But there's been an . . . incident."

Aunt Daisy glared at George.

"I'm so sorry, Henry," she said in an exasperated voice. "My nephew here just can't seem to stay out of trouble!"

"Oh, no, ma'am!" Henry exclaimed. "This has nothing to do with George. It's the ship, ma'am. Seems we've bumped an iceberg. I'm sure the captain is just being cautious, but he wants everyone up on deck."

"It's after midnight," Aunt Daisy said with a laugh. "Surely the captain doesn't expect us to appear on deck in our nightclothes!"

"No, ma'am. It's very cold outside." Henry walked over to the dresser and brought out three life jackets. "And you'll need to put these on. Over your coats."

Aunt Daisy stared at the life jackets as if Henry was holding up clown costumes.

"Henry! I'm not taking the children out into the cold for some kind of drill! Has Captain Smith lost his senses?"

"Of course not, Mrs. Key," Henry said. "Now

if you could get yourself and the children ready. I'll be back in just a moment to see if you need any help."

He left them alone.

"All right, George," Aunt Daisy said. "I guess we'll have another adventure to boast about when we get back. You get dressed. I'll get Phoebe up."

Aunt Daisy went to Phoebe's bed, pulling aside the curtains.

George heard a gasp, and he rushed over.

Phoebe wasn't there.

"Where could she be?" Aunt Daisy exclaimed.

A cold feeling crept up George's spine. Phoebe, his guardian angel. She must have woken up while George was gone, and now she was somewhere on the ship. Searching for George.

He took a deep breath.

"I went out exploring," George said. "After you went to bed. I didn't think Phoebe would wake up. She never does!"

"So she's out there looking for you?" Aunt Daisy said.

George nodded. "She doesn't want me getting into trouble." He kept his eyes glued to the floor. Aunt Daisy should be furious with him, and Papa was right! George had no sense. Not one lick of sense.

How would they ever find Phoebe?

But then George had an idea . . . that lemon drop in the hallway.

Could it be?

He ran out into the corridor, which was still empty. It seemed Henry wasn't having much luck getting people out of bed and up onto the deck.

George ran a little ways down the hall.

There!

He hurried down a bit farther.

Yes! Another lemon drop!

Phoebe! His smart sister!

Aunt Daisy came up behind him.

"She's left a trail of lemon drops," George said.

Aunt Daisy looked confused.

"Like Hansel and Gretel," George explained. "She left a trail so she could find her way back."

CHAPTER 10

George and Aunt Daisy scrambled to get dressed and put on their life jackets. Aunt Daisy brought Phoebe's warmest coat, and George carried the extra life jacket. They'd quickly find Phoebe and head up to the boat deck. And tomorrow morning this would be a big joke to laugh at over breakfast.

George thought that Phoebe had gone to the promenade deck — that she'd been woken up by the commotion with the ice and figured that George had gone out to see what was happening.

But when they got to the main staircase, he saw that the yellow glints were headed downstairs, not up to the deck.

His heart sank.

Phoebe had headed down to the first class baggage hold. Because she knew that George would want to see that mummy.

Of course she'd known.

Phoebe could read his mind.

A chill went through George's bones.

What if the scar-faced man was lurking in the baggage hold when Phoebe got there?

He ran faster down the stairs now. Aunt Daisy called after him, but he didn't slow down.

But when he got down to G deck, there was a gate stretched across the doorway.

"This wasn't here when I came down," he said to Aunt Daisy. He tried to pull it open, but it was locked. And just on the other side there was

a mob of people standing restlessly, third class passengers from the looks of their worn clothing.

"Look," Aunt Daisy said, pointing at one of Phoebe's candies glinting on the floor on the other side of the gate, pushed next to the wall. "She's down here. Pardon me!" she called to the steward standing in front of the crowd.

"You've gone the wrong way, madam," he said, staring at Aunt Daisy's huge diamond ring. "The captain wants first class passengers up on the boat deck now."

"My niece is down here somewhere," Aunt Daisy said. "You need to let us through."

"I'm sure she wouldn't have wandered down this far," the steward said.

"We're quite sure she's down here," Aunt Daisy said. "So if you'll please open the gate."

"I'm sorry, madam," he said. "Regulations . . ."

"Open this gate at once!" Aunt Daisy shouted in a tone George had never heard her use before.

The man took a key from his pocket and opened the gate. He stepped aside to let them pass. The crowd surged forward.

"Get back!" the steward shouted. "We'll tell you when it's time for you to go up!"

A few of the men lunged toward him.

Aunt Daisy grabbed George's arm.

The steward took a pistol from his pocket. His hand shook as he waved it toward the crowd. George and Aunt Daisy stepped through the gate. The steward slammed it behind them.

They were trapped down there, just like everyone else.

George and Aunt Daisy squeezed through the crowd, weaving around trunks and stepping over sleeping children. There were so many people. If Phoebe's candies were down here, they couldn't see them anymore.

Suddenly something crashed into George from behind. A pair of arms wrapped around his waist so tightly he couldn't breathe.

George's heart stopped — the scar-faced man?

"GIORGIO!" Enzo screamed up at him.

George's eardrums nearly split in two.

Enzo's father hurried over to them. He tried to gently peel Enzo away from George.

But the little boy wouldn't let go.

"NO!" he howled. "NO!"

"Very sorry," Marco said, smiling apologetically at Aunt Daisy, who looked more confused than ever. "We are old friends of Giorgio."

George started to introduce Aunt Daisy, but before he could get three words out, Enzo was dragging him down the hall, elbowing his way through the crowd like a pint-sized bull.

"See! See!" Enzo said.

"What?" George said. "No . . ."

"See! See!"

What was this kid doing? What did he want George to see?

The answer was just a few steps away, through an open doorway.

It was the mail sorting room.

Except now all George could see was water, green water swirling halfway up the stairs, foaming and churning like a stormy river. Sacks of mail bobbed up and down. Hundreds of letters floated on the surface.

And now George understood what Enzo was saying.

Sea.

The sea.

The *Titanic* was filling with water from the sea.

CHAPTER 11

Unsinkable.

Unsinkable.

George whispered those words like a prayer, over and over in his mind. He thought of Mr. Andrews, of how sure he was of this ship.

But the longer he stared at that water, that foaming green water, rising higher every second, the more certain he became: The *Titanic* was in trouble.

"We must go up," Marco said to Aunt Daisy. "We find a way."

But she shook her head, holding up Phoebe's bright blue coat and her life jacket.

"My niece, Phoebe," Aunt Daisy said. "She's down here. . . ."

George could see she was fighting back tears. George had never seen her look so sad and helpless, not even when Uncle Cliff died.

"She came down here looking for me," George said. "We can't find her."

Marco's amber eyes became very intent.

"An idea," he said. He knelt down and spoke to Enzo in Italian.

The boy smiled and nodded.

Then Marco hoisted the little boy up onto his shoulders.

Enzo took a huge breath and screamed,

"Phoebe!

"PHOEBE!"

People stopped talking and stared up at the boy with the foghorn voice.

"Phoebe!

"PHOEBE!"

As a hush fell over the crowd, George heard a faint voice.

"I'm here! I'm here!"

The crowd parted, and Phoebe appeared, her spectacles crooked, her face pale.

She staggered forward and threw her arms around George, burying her face in his chest.

"I found you," she whispered.

George didn't bother arguing over who did the finding. And anyway, his words were stuck in his throat. So he just held her tight.

It took some time for Phoebe to calm down enough to tell her story: that yes, she had been looking for George and heading for the baggage hold, that she got caught in the crowd of people rushing toward the back of the ship.

"It was like a stampede," she said.

As Phoebe talked, Aunt Daisy helped her into her coat and life jacket. Enzo held Phoebe's hand, like they were old friends. And the strange thing was that it felt that way, like they'd known Marco and Enzo forever. Maybe that's what happened when you got trapped in a flooding ship together.

George started to feel calmer with Phoebe close to him.

But then came a deep booming sound, a kind of groaning that echoed up all around them. At first George thought maybe the engines had started up again. But no, this wasn't the sound of the *Titanic*'s mighty engines.

The entire ship catapulted forward. People fell, toppling like dominoes. George was thrown into the wall. Screams and shouts echoed through the hallway. He managed to grab Enzo by the life jacket as he went sailing by him. Enzo just giggled as he fell into George's lap. To him this was a fun game. George hoped he never figured out that it wasn't.

"What was that?" Phoebe gasped, digging her fingers into George's arms.

Nobody answered.

But they all knew.

The *Titanic* was sinking.

"We will go up," Marco said.

"How?" Aunt Daisy said.

Phoebe grabbed George's hand.

"You, Georgie," she said.

"What?" George said.

"Phoebe's right," Aunt Daisy said. "You know the ship better than anyone." She turned to Marco. "He's explored every inch."

George couldn't believe it. They were counting on him?

But what if he made a mistake?

What if they all got lost?

"You can do it," Phoebe whispered.

And so George closed his eyes, picturing Mr. Andrews's blueprints in his mind.

And he remembered: the escape ladders.

He remembered what Mr. Andrews had told him: *The ladders are in the stokers' quarters, and they run up three decks.*

He pointed toward the front of the ship.

"This way," he said.

CHAPTER 12

There was no crowd here. Just abandoned trunks and suitcases.

And water. It was seeping into the hallway from under the doors of some of the cabins. No wonder those people were trying to push their way upstairs. They'd probably known right away that the ship was in trouble and the bottom decks were flooding.

The door to the stokers' quarters was locked.

Marco handed Enzo over to George and rammed the door with his shoulder, breaking the lock.

George rushed inside and went to the back wall.

And there it was, a ladder bolted to the wall. Just like Mr. Andrews said it would be. It came through the floor and shot straight up through an opening in the ceiling. George almost laughed with relief.

"Bravo, George!" Marco said.

"Bravo, Giorgio!" Enzo said, clapping.

George hopped up onto the ladder, with Phoebe and Aunt Daisy at his heels.

George was worried about Enzo, but the little guy scrambled like a monkey right ahead of Marco. They came up in a small dining room meant for crew members, and then George led everyone down a long second class corridor, up the grand staircase, and finally out onto the crowded boat deck.

They'd made it!

An officer came hurrying over to Aunt Daisy.

"Madam, there is a lifeboat about to leave. You and the children must come at once."

The man looked at Marco.

"Women and children only, sir," he said somberly. "I'm afraid you will have to stay with the other gentlemen."

Marco nodded. "Yes," he said. "I know."

Phoebe had been right. There weren't enough lifeboats. Not nearly enough.

What would happen to all of these men on deck? There were hundreds of them! And what about the crew? And those people down on G deck?

George's heart was pounding so hard he thought it would break through his chest.

He felt dizzy and sick.

Marco got down on his knees and spoke very quietly to Enzo.

Enzo nodded. Marco kissed him on the forehead, and then Enzo ran over to Aunt Daisy. She picked him up.

"I say he will go on a special boat ride," Marco said. "I say you will not leave him."

Aunt Daisy nodded, her eyes welling with tears.

"I promise you that."

Marco and Aunt Daisy looked at each other. Neither of them said a word, but a whole conversation seemed to happen with their eyes.

Phoebe was really crying now, looking away so Enzo wouldn't see. George felt like someone was choking him.

"Come on now!" the officer screamed.

And so they left Marco, and when George turned around just a few seconds later, he was gone.

The officer led them through a crowd of men to the side of the ship, where a lifeboat hung just over the side. It was packed with people, all women and children except for two sailors who stood at either end.

An officer helped Phoebe over the rail, and then one of the sailors reached over and pulled her into the boat. George helped Enzo, who tumbled in next to Phoebe. Aunt Daisy had a hard time climbing over in her skirts, but George held her hand, and she finally made it.

Now it was George's turn. As he took a step over the railing, someone pulled him back roughly.

"No more room," the officer said. "Women and children only. Lower away!" he called.

"No!" called Aunt Daisy, standing up in the boat. "He's only ten years old! Wait!"

The lifeboat rocked and almost tipped over. Ladies shrieked.

"You will drown us all!" a woman shouted.

"Sit down or I'll throw you over!" the sailor said.

And now Phoebe was screaming too.

Enzo howled.

George was too shocked to move.

Phoebe leaped up and grabbed hold of one of the ropes. She was trying to climb out of the lifeboat, back to George. He gasped as her hand slipped and she dangled over the sea. A sailor grabbed her around the waist and threw her into the boat.

And then the boat slid down on its ropes and splashed into the water.

Aunt Daisy and Phoebe were shouting up at him as the sailors rowed the boat away. George stood there at the rail, watching, his entire body shaking.

He stood there for what felt like a long time after their boat disappeared into the darkness.

He couldn't look down at the water, so he stared up at the sky, at all of those stars.

He closed his eyes and told himself it was a nightmare. He was really asleep in his suite. Or no, he was home on the farm, in his bed, with

Phoebe sleeping across the room and Papa sitting by the fire downstairs.

He closed his eyes tighter.

He tried to block out the terrible noises around him. He felt himself tipping to the side and he held tighter to the rail. And then he couldn't hold on anymore. His hand slipped.

And George fell, smashing his head on the deck.

And then there was silence.

CHAPTER 13

Strong arms lifted George up. He felt himself being carried.

"Papa?" he said. "Papa?"

Why did his head hurt so much? Had the panther knocked him out of the tree? Was he sick with a fever like Mama? And whose voice was whispering in his ear?

"Giorgio. Giorgio. Wake up."

George opened his eyes. Marco's amber eyes shone down on him.

This was no dream. He was not sick.

The *Titanic* was sinking.

The bow was completely underwater now, and waves swept over the deck. Lounge chairs sailed past them and crashed over the side. People clung to the rails. A few slipped and were swept overboard.

Marco had wrapped one arm around the railing and the other around George.

"It's time to go," Marco said.

"Go where?" George said, even though he knew.

They were going into the water. There was nowhere else for them to go.

Marco held George's arm as they climbed over the railing.

"When we jump, jump as far out as you can," Marco said. "Away from the ship."

George filled his lungs with the icy air.

"Jump!" Marco cried.

George pushed with his feet and leaped off the

boat. He closed his eyes, imagining that he had enormous wings that would take him soaring into the sky.

But then he hit the water, and down he went.

And just when he was sure his lungs would pop, the ocean seemed to spit him back up. George sputtered. The water was so cold it felt like millions of needles were stabbing him. It hurt so much he couldn't move.

Someone grabbed him by the life jacket and started dragging him away from the ship. It took George a few seconds to realize that it was Marco. He stopped to grab a door that was floating by. After helping George climb up on top, Marco found a crate for himself. It wasn't big enough to keep his feet out of the water. But it was better than nothing. The crate had a rope attached to it. Marco tied it around his arm and handed the end to George.

"Hold tight," he said.

They turned and stared at the ship.

The entire front was underwater, and the back had risen toward the sky. It groaned and squeaked and sparked. Black smoke poured from its funnels, and the lights flickered. It was like watching a fairy-tale dragon, stabbed and bleeding, fighting for its life.

And finally it seemed to give up.

The groaning stopped. The lights went dark. And the *Titanic* sank into the bubbling black water, down, down, down, down, until George closed his eyes.

He couldn't make himself watch Mr. Andrews's beautiful ship disappear.

A sound rose up around him, people calling for help. More and more people, screaming and yelling, hundreds of voices swirling together like a howling wind.

Marco pulled George away from the people and the wreckage. George couldn't believe how

strong he was, how hard he kicked, how his arms sliced through the water.

When he finally stopped, Marco was gasping for breath, exhaling cold clouds of white mist. He tightened the rope around his arm and patted George on the shoulder.

"I rest now, Giorgio," he said breathlessly. He closed his eyes and put his head down on the crate. "Soon."

Soon what? George was afraid to ask. Soon it would be over? Soon they would be rescued? Or soon they would be swallowed up by the darkness?

George heard men talking somewhere close by.

He looked around, relieved that he wasn't all by himself, and to his shock, just ahead, he saw a lifeboat.

"Marco!" he said. "Wake up!"

But Marco didn't move. His arms hung off the side of the crate. His feet dangled in the icy water.

"Marco! We need to get to that boat!"

But Marco was still. And George realized that his friend had used every last ounce of strength. He'd gotten George off the sinking ship, and across the icy waters.

It was up to George now.

He tucked the rope under his body and started paddling. The water seared his hands and arms. It was so cold it felt boiling hot, like lava.

But he didn't stop until he reached the boat.

It wasn't a regular wooden lifeboat. It was much smaller, and made of canvas cloth. There were about ten people crowded inside, mostly men. They all seemed dazed and frozen. Nobody spoke as George paddled up and grabbed hold of the side.

But somebody pushed his hand off.

"Get back," a voice said weakly. "You'll put us all in the water."

"Please," George said. "We need help."

George put his hand up again, but again someone pushed it off.

And so George pulled Marco to the other side of the boat. He tried again.

Nobody helped him. But this time nobody stopped him.

It took him three tries, but he managed to hoist himself over the side and tumble into the boat.

And now for Marco.

He got up on his knees and leaned over, bracing his legs against the side of the boat as he grabbed Marco under the arms. He pulled, but Marco was attached to the crate by the rope. He tried again, yanking the rope, digging at the knot with his frozen fingers. But the knot was like rusted metal. George struggled, and water sloshed over the side of the boat.

"Just let him go," one of the men said weakly. "It's hopeless."

But George kept working on the rope, trying now to break it away from the crate. He was pulling so hard that at first he didn't notice that Marco was slipping into the sea.

"Please! Somebody!" George screamed. "Can't you help us?"

A woman from the front of the boat climbed back to George.

She wore a black coat, her head and face hidden by a flowered shawl. As she pushed George aside she pulled something out of her coat.

A knife!

With a clean cut, she sliced the rope and helped George pull Marco into the boat.

Her hands looked surprisingly strong.

George fell back, exhausted.

"Thank you," George said to the woman through his chattering teeth.

The woman didn't say anything, and suddenly George noticed the knife. A bowie knife with an elk-horn handle.

George looked up, under the shawl. Two glittering blue eyes looked back at him.

The scar-faced man.

He had saved Marco's life.

Without a word, he handed George his knife.

Then he looked away.

CHAPTER 14

The cold pressed down on George until it seemed to crush his bones. He huddled close to Marco, trying to keep them both warm. Marco barely moved.

Some of the men sang softly.

Others prayed.

Some made no sounds at all.

Hours went by.

The sea became rougher, and every few minutes a wave splashed into the boat.

George was drifting off to sleep when one of the men shouted.

"It's a ship!"

And sure enough, a bright light was heading toward them.

"No," another man said. "It's just lightning."

But the light was getting bigger. And brighter.

George stared at that light, afraid that if he even blinked it would disappear, but soon he could see the outline of a gigantic ship steaming toward them.

He whispered to Marco, who barely fluttered his eyes. He pulled his friend closer, rubbing his arms.

"It won't be long," he whispered. "Hang on."

As the sky brightened, George gaped at the scene around him. It was as if they'd fallen through a hole in the ocean and come out on the other side of the earth.

There were icebergs all around them — hundreds of them, as far as George could see.

They sparkled in the golden pink light. They were so beautiful, but looking at them sent a chill up George's spine.

As the ship got closer, George could see that it was a passenger steamer, like the *Titanic*. Closer and closer it came, until George could read its name: *Carpathia*.

There were people crowded on the deck, looking over the rail. They were yelling and shouting and waving. But one voice rose above all the others, like a siren:

"PAPA! PAPA! GIORGIO!"

Marco's eyes fluttered, and he smiled a little.

"Enzo," he whispered.

George could see the little boy, waving frantically from Aunt Daisy's arms. Phoebe stood next to them, waving, with the sunlight glinting off her spectacles.

"They're safe, Marco!" George said. "They made it!"

George grabbed Marco's hand.

"And so did we."

CHAPTER 15

Those first two days on the *Carpathia* were a blur.

George mostly slept, on a bed of blankets and pillows on the floor of the first class lounge. But he sensed that Phoebe and Aunt Daisy never left his side. He sometimes heard Enzo singing softly to him in Italian, his breath hot on George's cheek. He heard Aunt Daisy and Phoebe talking—about Marco, whose feet were badly frozen, about the *Carpathia*'s passengers, who couldn't do enough for them all. About the hundreds and hundreds of people who didn't make it out of the water.

Slowly George felt stronger, and on their last night at sea, he was able to go out onto the deck with Phoebe.

They sat on a bench, wrapped in a blanket. A stewardess came over and gave them each a mug of warm milk.

Phoebe looked up at the sky as she warmed her hands on her mug.

"I finally saw a shooting star, when I was on the lifeboat," she said. "You can guess what I wished for."

George reached for her hand.

Yes, of course he knew.

On the bench next to them sat two women. Both were crying. Probably they'd lost their husbands. Or brothers. Or fathers.

There hadn't been enough wishing stars for everyone that night.

Phoebe said that only about 700 of them made it out of the water.

Phoebe leaned in close to George. Her coat smelled like rose water. A lady from the *Carpathia* had given it to her.

"Have you wondered?" she asked quietly, "if maybe there really was a curse?"

At first George didn't understand that Phoebe was talking about the mummy.

With all that had happened, George hadn't thought about it.

But now it hit him: how strange it was that the ship had collided with the iceberg at the exact moment the scar-faced man had opened the lid of Mr. Burrows's crate.

"I guess we'll never know," George said.

But the next evening, as the *Carpathia* was closing in on New York Harbor, George and Phoebe overheard a skinny man with a beard speaking to an officer.

"Before the *Titanic*, I was traveling in Egypt, a

place called Thebes," the man said. "I explored a magnificent tomb of a royal family."

Phoebe's eyes bugged out.

And before George could stop her, she had marched over to the man.

"Excuse me," she said. "Are you Mr. Burrows?"

"Yes, I am," the man replied.

Phoebe took a big breath.

"Mr. Burrows," she said. "This might sound like a very strange question. But did you bring a mummy on board the *Titanic*?"

The man looked at Phoebe.

"A mummy?" he said.

"Yes," she said. "We heard it was a princess."

Mr. Burrows's eyes were tired and sad.

But he smiled a little.

"My princess," he said. "Yes."

"So there *was* a mummy?" Phoebe exclaimed.

"No, child," he said. "One should never take a mummy from a tomb. That is very bad luck.

Princess was my cat. She passed away on my trip to Egypt. And so I had her . . . wrapped, so I could bring her back with me."

"So the princess was a cat?"

"Yes," he said sadly. "The most beautiful cat that ever lived."

Three hours later, just after nine o'clock, the *Carpathia* docked in New York City in a thunderstorm.

There were thousands of people waiting on the pier.

But the first person George saw as they walked down the gangplank was Papa. He rushed up to George and Phoebe, grabbing them both and pulling them to him. All around them, people cried with happiness. Others just cried, their tears mixing with the pouring rain.

They introduced Papa to Marco and Enzo, but there wasn't much time to talk. Their train to

Millerstown was leaving soon, and an ambulance was waiting to take Marco to the hospital.

Luckily, George didn't have to say a real good-bye to Marco and Enzo.

Aunt Daisy was staying in New York City to take care of Enzo until Marco's feet were healed. And then they would come with her for a visit to Millerstown. Seeing the way Marco and Aunt Daisy were looking at each other, George wondered if maybe Marco and Enzo would stay forever. George sure hoped so.

As they rode to the train station, newsboys screamed from every street corner.

"Read all about it! Titanic *survivors in New York! More than fifteen hundred people dead! Read all about it!"*

George covered his ears.

He wanted to forget everything about the *Titanic.*

He wanted to put it out of his mind forever.

CHAPTER 16

But he couldn't forget.

Even back on the farm, surrounded by friends from school and neighbors from town, he felt like he was still drifting on the dark ocean. And each day that went by, he felt himself drifting farther away. At night, when he got into bed, he'd see the faces of all those scared people on G deck. He'd see the ship disappearing into the sea. He'd remember the stabbing cold, and the screams of hundreds of people crying for help.

He didn't bother trying to fall asleep. Each night, after Phoebe and Papa were in bed, he went out into the woods.

He was heading back to the house one night when he heard a noise through the bushes.

Something was there. He could sense it.

The panther?

He took out his knife, fighting the urge to run away, and peered through the branches.

George stared in shock.

It was Papa.

He was sitting on a large rock, looking up at the sky, smoking his pipe. He looked like he'd been there for some time.

Papa turned. He didn't look especially surprised to see George.

"Sorry to give you a scare," he said.

"What are you doing here?" George asked.

"Don't know," Papa said. "Sometimes I just come here, when I can't sleep."

George couldn't believe it. How many nights

had they both been out in the woods at the same time?

Papa eased himself off the rock and began walking back toward the house. "I'll take you up to your bed."

"No, Papa," George said. "I come to the woods too."

Papa looked at him with a very slight smile.

"I know that," he said.

Papa knew? What else did Papa know about George?

What else *didn't* George know about Papa?

He and and his father looked at each other. Really looked, for the first time in a long while, maybe since Mama died.

Suddenly George started to cry. They took him by surprise, his tears, and he couldn't stop. He cried for all those people who didn't make it out of the water. He cried because somehow he did. He cried because he knew that no matter how much time went by, a part of him would still be out in that ocean. He would never forget.

Papa held George's hand and didn't say a word. And then he led George over to the boulder, where they sat together under the stars.

George stared up at the sky. Were those really the same stars that had burned so brightly above the black ocean that night?

Was he really still the same boy?

George, who couldn't stay out of trouble. George, who didn't try hard at school.

George, who found the escape ladders. George, who pulled Marco to that lifeboat.

Who didn't give up.

They sat on the boulder for a long while, and as the sun started to peep over the trees, George told Papa about Mr. Andrews.

"He said he thought one day I'd build a ship."

Papa didn't laugh. He puffed on his pipe, looking thoughtful.

"How about we build one together?" Papa said. "A nice little boat. For the pond. I've always wanted to do that."

"That's a good idea," George said.

A great idea.

"We could start today," Papa said, standing up and holding out his hand.

They walked back to the house together. The birds were singing softly. The chickens were squawking for breakfast. A breeze was whispering through the trees. And a voice seemed to sing to George, very softly:

"Awake, awake.
It's now daybreak!
But don't forget your dreams. . . ."

Papa looked out into the woods, like he could hear it too.

MY *TITANIC* STORY

This book is a work of historical fiction. That means that all of the facts about the *Titanic* are true, but the main characters came from my imagination. George, Phoebe, Aunt Daisy, Marco, and Enzo are based on people I learned about while researching the *Titanic*. By the time I finished writing this book, they sure felt real to me.

I can see George now, relaxing in the little boat he and Papa built, rowing around their pond while Phoebe watches from the shore, reading a book about dinosaur fossils. I can picture Aunt Daisy and Marco's wedding, how Enzo would run down the aisle with a huge grin on his face. That's my favorite part of being a writer, giving my characters happiness in the end. If only I could do the same for the 1,517 people who didn't survive the sinking of the *Titanic*.

What a sad and terrible story!

One day as I was trying to finish the book, I needed a break, so I went to New York City with my eleven-year-old son, Dylan. We stopped to rest in one of my favorite neighborhoods, in a tiny park on West 106th Street and Broadway with trees and a bronze statue of a woman lying on her side. I read the gold writing engraved in a marble bench, and to my surprise I saw that the entire park was a memorial to two famous New Yorkers who died on the *Titanic*, Isidor and Ida Straus.

I couldn't forget the *Titanic*, it seemed, not even for an afternoon.

And nearly one hundred years later, the world hasn't forgotten either.

FACTS ABOUT THE *TITANIC*

More has been written about the *Titanic* than any other disaster in modern history. I tried to include as much information as I could in the book. But here are some more amazing facts that I wanted to share with you.

- The *Titanic* was the largest ship—the largest moving object—ever built. It weighed close to 50,000 tons, and was eleven stories tall and four city blocks long.

- There were 2,229 people on board—1,316 passengers and 913 crew. Survivors included 498 passengers and 215 members of the crew.

- The passengers came from 28 different countries, including many from America, England, Ireland, and

Finland. There were a few passengers from China, Japan, Mexico, and South Africa. Most of the crew members were from England and Ireland.

- There were nine dogs on the *Titanic*. They stayed in kennels, but their owners could take them out onto the decks for walks. Two Pomeranians and one Pekingese survived with their masters.

- After the sinking of the *Titanic*, laws were changed to require all ships to carry enough lifeboats for every passenger and crew member.

- For decades, divers, scientists, and treasure hunters searched for the wreck of the *Titanic*. It was finally located in 1985 by a team led by U.S. scientist Robert Ballard, 2 1/2 miles below the surface of the sea.

- Ballard and his team did not take anything from the wreck. Dr. Ballard believes the *Titanic* should rest in peace as a memorial to those who died. But he couldn't stop treasure hunters from diving to the wreck and removing thousands of artifacts: jewelry, dishes, clothes, even the ship's hull.

What do you think about this? Do you think the *Titanic* should be brought to the surface or left in peace?

THE NEW YORK TIMES BESTSELLING SERIES
I SURVIVED
THE SHARK ATTACKS OF 1916
by Lauren Tarshis
SCHOLASTIC

I SURVIVED

THE SHARK ATTACKS OF 1916

by Lauren Tarshis

illustrated by Scott Dawson

Scholastic Inc.

CHAPTER 1

A feeling of terror came over ten-year-old Chet Roscow, a chill deep down in his bones. He had been swimming in the Matawan Creek by himself. But he had the idea that someone — or something — was watching him.

And then he saw it — a large gray fin, slicing

through the water like a knife. What was that? Could it really be . . .

A shark?

That was impossible! Elm Hills was miles and miles from the ocean. How could a shark find its way into this little creek?

There was no way. . . .

But now Chet could see it, coming toward him.

The gigantic shark, bigger than Chet himself. The black eyes staring up through the water.

Killer eyes.

Chet dove toward the shore, pounding through the water, kicking with all his might. His feet touched the bottom. He was running now, looking over his shoulder. The shark was right behind him, its huge jaws wide open, its white dagger teeth gleaming in its bloodred mouth.

CHAPTER 2

NINE DAYS EARLIER...

JULY 3, 1916

9:00 A.M.

THE ELM HILLS DINER

The Monday morning breakfast rush at the Elm Hills Diner was finally over.

Chet's feet ached. He was covered in syrup, doughnut crumbs, and bacon grease. His curly red hair was damp with sweat. But he was surprisingly happy. Uncle Jerry was paying him a fortune to help out at his diner this summer — fifteen cents a day! Chet liked being surrounded by familiar faces and hearing folks calling out his name while he worked. Best of all, he was finally making some friends, his first since he came to live with Uncle Jerry last January. He was staying here for the year, while Mama and Papa were in California on business.

Chet was wiping down the counter when the front door banged open.

He smiled when he saw Dewey, Sid, and Monty rushing toward him. They came in every morning on their way to work at the tile factory. Chet had seen them at school — the loud boys who were always talking about baseball. But he hadn't gotten to know them until this summer.

"Did you hear?" Dewey said, his freckly cheeks red with excitement.

"You won't believe it!" said Monty, whose spectacles were fogged up from the humidity.

"Let me tell him!" said Sid, pushing his friends aside. He was the shortest of the three, and always in charge. "It was a shark!"

And then they all started talking at once.

"A shark attack!"

"It was huge!"

"Bit off a man's leg!"

"There was blood everywhere!"

"The man is dead!"

"It happened right in Beach Haven!" said Monty.

Beach Haven was about seventy miles south of Elm Hills, right on the Atlantic Ocean. Chet had heard about the fine hotels there, and the people who swam in the ocean in their fancy bathing costumes. But he'd never heard of any shark attacks!

Uncle Jerry appeared from the kitchen, his bright blue eyes shining and his thick dark hair neatly combed back.

The guys always stood a little straighter when

they saw Chet's uncle. He'd been a baseball legend growing up here in Elm Hills. He could have gone pro, but he'd hurt his knee sliding home in a championship game. The team won, and Uncle Jerry could never play again. He still limped a little after a long day of work.

"What's this about a shark?" he said as he passed out cinnamon doughnuts to each of the boys. "You fellas aren't trying to fool us, are you?"

Chet knew the guys loved to pull pranks. On the last day of school, they'd put a frog in Minnie Marston's lunch pail. She was the prettiest girl in school, but she'd been so mad her face turned an ugly shade of purple.

"We're not foolin'!" Monty said, pulling a rumpled piece of newsprint from his trouser pocket. "Look at this!" he said.

He handed it to Chet. It was from the *New Jersey Herald*. The hair on the back of Chet's

neck stood up as he read the story. Uncle Jerry read it over his shoulder.

KILLER SHARK ATTACKS SWIMMER!

JULY 2, 1916
BEACH HAVEN, NEW JERSEY

Charles Vansant, 25, was attacked by a large shark Saturday, July 1, while swimming in chest-deep water. He and his family were vacationing at the luxurious Engleside Hotel.

Mr. Vansant, known by all as a man of exceptional charm and great promise, was swimming with a dog when the attack occurred. The beach was filled with fashionable ladies and gentlemen enjoying the early evening breezes, when panicked shouts suddenly echoed through the air. A large black fin could be seen swimming toward Mr. Vansant. Onlookers screamed warnings. But it was too late. The shark brutally attacked the young man, who struggled to swim to shore. A lifeguard and two men rushed to his aid and finally managed to free him from the water.

But he died a short time later of his injuries. This is the first fatal shark attack on a human ever recorded on the northeastern shore of the United States.

Uncle Jerry laughed.

Chet stared at him. His uncle was tough. But did he really think a man getting ripped apart by a shark was funny?

"Boys, that article is a hoax," Uncle Jerry said. "A shark will not attack a human. It's a proven fact. Haven't you ever heard of Mr. Hermann Oelrichs?"

None of them had.

"The guy was a millionaire," Uncle Jerry said. "Owned a big shipping company. One day — let's see, I think it was about twenty-five years ago — this gent was out on his yacht with his rich friends, not far from New York City. They were out in the ocean, and they sailed right into a big school of sharks. The ladies screamed. But Oelrichs put on his bathing costume and dove into the water, practically right on top of those sharks."

"Why did he do that?" Sid said.

"To prove that the sharks wouldn't attack," Uncle Jerry said. "He made a real commotion, splashing and kicking, even shouting at the sharks. And wouldn't you know, the sharks swam away. They were scared as rabbits."

Sid glanced at Chet and smiled.

"And that's not all!" said Uncle Jerry. "Mr. Oelrichs offered a five-hundred-dollar reward to anyone who could come up with one case of a shark attacking a human on the northeastern coast of the United States."

"Five hundred bucks!" said Dewey. "That's crazy!"

"Maybe," Uncle Jerry said. "But nobody ever

collected. Because a shark simply will not attack a human. That cherry pie over there is more likely to attack you than a shark is."

They all laughed.

But then a gravelly voice spoke up from the end of the counter.

"You got it wrong. Some sharks are killers."

It was Captain Wilson, who came into the diner every day for breakfast. A long time ago he had been a whaling ship captain. But now he puttered around the creek in his broken-down motorboat. Usually he had a dazed look in his eyes, like he wasn't sure where he was.

But now the Captain's eyes were sharp.

"You've seen some sharks, Cap?" Uncle Jerry said, refilling the Captain's coffee cup.

"Seen one?" the Captain said. "A white shark almost bit me right in two."

"That so?" Uncle Jerry said, winking at Chet.

"I don't want to scare you lads," the Captain said.

"Please, sir!" Monty said. "Nothing scares us."

"We can take it!" Sid insisted.

Chet realized with a happy jolt that the "we" included him.

Uncle Jerry went back into the kitchen, shaking his head.

"All right then," the Captain said, looking around the empty diner. "But gather close. And don't scream too loud. I don't want to upset the other customers."

CHAPTER 3

"The year was 1852," the Captain began. "I wasn't much older than you lads. It was one of my first whaling voyages. Two years at sea, and finally I was heading home across the Pacific."

His voice was low and whispery, like it was coming from someplace very far away.

"Suddenly, the sky turned black. The wind started to howl, and rain poured down. I'll never forget those waves. I thought our ship was going to be tossed to the moon. And the wind! It ripped our ship apart, like it was made of paper. We all went into the water. I grabbed a barrel and somehow I made it through the night. By the time the sun came up, the storm had passed. I was all alone. Just a tiny speck in the middle of the ocean."

"The other men died?" Dewey asked.

But the Captain didn't seem to hear.

"And then I saw the fin."

"The shark?" whispered Monty, edging a little closer to Sid.

"Shhhh," Sid said.

"It circled me for a long while," the Captain said. "Around and around, real slow, like he was toying with me. Little by little, it came closer, and closer. Until I could see its eyes.

"Black as coal," he whispered. "Killer eyes."

The Captain was looking out the window now, like he expected to see that shark with its open jaws pressed against the glass.

"Killer eyes," he repeated quietly.

It was a minute before he started talking again. The guys waited with their tongues practically hanging out.

"The beast went underwater, and for a second

I thought maybe it'd decided I wasn't worth the trouble. But then something bumped me in the leg. Scraped me bloody! The skin of a shark is rough. You can use it as sandpaper."

The Captain rubbed his leg like it still hurt.

"It came in for the kill with its jaws wide open," the Captain said. "Big enough to swallow me whole. And the teeth. Like daggers, a thousand daggers, all lined up in rows."

The Captain's hands were shaking now.

"I had an old harpoon tip in my pocket. I grabbed it. And I stabbed the shark." He pounded the counter so hard that his coffee mug crashed to the floor. The Captain didn't notice.

"Right in its killer eye," he said.

"You killed it?" Dewey said.

The Captain shook his head. "Oh, no," he said. "But it swam off. Disappeared. It wasn't my time."

Then he stood up and put on his tattered captain's hat.

"I must get home now," he said. "My sweet Deborah will be waiting for me."

Deborah was his wife. She'd been dead for at least twenty years.

Chet and the guys watched him leave.

Uncle Jerry had come out of the kitchen when he heard the crash of the Captain's cup.

"Poor old guy," he said, as he swept up the mess. "His mind is like Swiss cheese."

"You mean that story isn't true?" Monty asked.

Uncle Jerry shrugged. "I think the Captain spins a mighty fine tale."

"Stabbed it with a harpoon tip!" Dewey laughed.

"Killer eyes!" Monty barked.

"Next the Captain will be telling us he got gobbled up by a whale," Sid said.

Still, Chet thought about the Captain all day. He didn't really believe the story either. Uncle Jerry was right. Whoever heard of a shark attacking a person?

No, it wasn't the shark that scared him. It was the idea of being alone in the middle of the ocean. Strange, but Chet could imagine that feeling. He'd been traveling around the country with Mama and Papa most of his life. Papa was always chasing some new business idea. Selling motorcars in Oregon. Building bicycles in St. Louis. Taking family portraits in Philadelphia. Mama would get them settled into an apartment or a run-down little house. Chet would try to make friends. And just when they were starting to get comfortable, the business would go bad or Papa would get some other idea. "We're hitting the road," Papa would announce. And Mama would have to start packing again.

Chet was supposed to go along to California,

where Papa was sure he'd finally strike it rich. But then Mama decided that Chet would stay with Uncle Jerry instead.

"It's a nice town," Mama had said. "And Uncle Jerry will take good care of you."

Chet remembered all the fun he used to have with Uncle Jerry when he was little, how Uncle Jerry had taught him how to throw a baseball. But they hadn't seen each other in years. Would his uncle even recognize him after all this time?

He shouldn't have worried. Uncle Jerry was standing on the train platform when Chet got off, a huge grin on his face. "It's about time," he said to Chet, wrapping him up in a hug that went on until after the train pulled out of the station. From that first day, Uncle Jerry made him feel right at home.

But Chet missed Mama and Papa. And it didn't matter how much he loved being with Uncle Jerry, or how many people shouted "Hiya, Chet!" when they came into the diner.

Soon enough he'd have to join Mama and Papa in California.

Would he ever really belong anywhere?

Or would he always be on his own, a tiny speck in the middle of the ocean?

CHAPTER 4

That next week was so hot, horses were fainting up and down Main Street. By Thursday, the temperature inside the diner was 102 degrees. But Chet didn't mind the heat. Something amazing had happened that day: The guys had invited Chet to go swimming with them at the creek.

All week they'd been coming into the diner earlier and earlier, and then sticking around even after they'd wolfed down their doughnuts.

"You ever seen the Pacific Ocean?" Sid had asked one day.

"Sure," Chet said.

"What's it look like?" Monty asked.

Chet took a minute to picture it. He didn't want to disappoint the guys.

"A little bluer than the Atlantic. Waves a little bigger maybe. But otherwise just lots of water and waves."

They all seemed satisfied.

"How about the Mississippi River?" Dewey had asked the next day. "You seen that too?"

Chet told them it was wide and muddy.

"I was on a steamboat that got stuck in the mud," Chet said. "We had to stay there for a whole day and night."

That impressed them all.

"You're the luckiest kid I know," Sid pronounced.

"Me?" Chet said.

"Sure!" Monty said. "To see all those places!"

"I don't know," Chet said. "I hate moving around so much."

Hearing those words startled Chet. He felt that way, but he'd never said it out loud. Not even to Uncle Jerry. He hoped the guys didn't think he was bellyaching.

"Hey, why don't you ever come down to the creek?" Sid said.

"We're always looking for you there," Monty said.

Chet tried to hide his surprise.

"It's not the Pacific Ocean," Dewey said. "But it's pretty nice."

"I hear it's better than the Pacific," Chet said.

The guys all laughed.

"Why don't you come today?" Sid said, and of course Chet said he would meet them after work.

Uncle Jerry drew Chet a little map so he wouldn't get lost—a dotted line to the end of Main Street, and then behind the tile factory. Down a steep hill and across a path.

Chet made it to the bottom of the hill, and for a second he thought he was lost. He couldn't see the creek, just tall golden grass. But then he could hear shouts and splashing. He walked through the grass and into a clearing. The guys' dusty trousers and shirts were laid across some low branches. Three pairs of scuffed-up boots were tumbled across the dirt.

And just beyond, there was the creek.

The guys were right: It wasn't much—maybe twenty feet across. He couldn't tell if it was deep enough to dive. But it was nice and shady, and at that moment there was no place on earth that Chet would rather be.

"Hurry up!" Dewey shouted. "The water's perfect."

Chet threw his clothes off and climbed up onto the broken-down dock.

"Jump!" Sid said.

With a running leap, Chet launched himself into the air.

Whoosh! The cool water rose up around him. All of his worries washed away.

The guys gathered around him. Dewey threw a pink rubber ball high into the air.

"Chet! Catch!" he said.

Chet squinted up into the sun and, miraculously, caught the ball.

"Here!" Sid yelled, jumping up and waving his hands. Chet threw the ball, straight enough, like Uncle Jerry had taught him. Sid made a clean catch.

They played ball, then they took turns jumping off the dock and chasing each other back and forth across the creek.

When they got tired of swimming, they sat on

the bank under a big elm tree. Dewey's mother had packed him three big molasses cookies, and the guys fought over who could share with Chet.

"So?" Sid said. "You like it here okay?"

"The creek's nice," said Chet with a mouth full of cookie.

"No, Elm Hills," Monty said.

"You think you'll be staying a while?" said Dewey.

Chet swallowed hard. Just the day before, he'd gotten a letter from Mama. *"We have a nice apartment with a room just for you,"* she wrote. *"I think Papa is going to have some good luck this time."*

"I hope," he said.

The guys all nodded.

"Minnie Marston's sweet on you," Dewey said.

"Really?" Chet squeaked.

"Sure," Monty said, sounding a little jealous. "She told my sister."

They sat there a while, talking about Minnie, and Uncle Jerry's no-hitter in the high school finals of 1908. Then Sid stood up and dove back into the water. They all followed him.

Sid went swimming down the creek, and Chet played ball with Dewey and Monty. He and Monty tossed the ball back and forth a few times.

"Dewey!" Chet called, ready to throw the ball.

But Dewey didn't look at him. He was looking at something downstream. He had a strange look on his face.

And then Chet saw it too: a gray triangle sticking up through the water, heading right for Dewey.

What was that?

It looked like the fin of a giant fish. Was it . . .

He shook his head. His eyes were playing tricks on him.

A shark in the creek was impossible.

He even tried to laugh. His mind must be messed up because of the Captain's story.

But the fin was getting closer to Dewey. Faster, faster, closer, closer.

"Dewey!" Chet shouted.

But it was too late.

There was a huge splash. And then Dewey disappeared.

CHAPTER 5

Chet ran screaming out of the water. "Dewey! Dewey!"

He made it to the bank and searched the water for Monty and Sid, but they were gone too.

They'd been eaten! Chet was the only one left! He was about to run up to Main Street for help, but then Dewey came up sputtering.

"You idiot," Dewey said, looking around. "You kept me under too long! That wasn't the plan!"

Who was Dewey talking to? And what did he mean about a *plan*?

Sid came up out of the water, gasping for breath. Where was the shark? And why was Sid laughing?

"We got you!" Sid shouted at Chet. He held something up.

A chipped gray tile.

The fin.

Chet's head started to spin. He felt like he might throw up. They'd tricked him!

Monty was standing on the bank on the other side of the creek. "I can't believe you fell for that!" he laughed.

Chet couldn't talk. His heart seemed to be stuck in his throat. Why would they do that?

"You should have heard yourself!" Monty shouted. "You screamed so loud! Your mama probably heard you all the way in California."

Chet's cheeks were bright red. His hands were shaking. How could he have thought these guys wanted to be his friends? They just wanted someone to pick on. That was the only reason they'd invited him to the creek.

Chet grabbed his clothes and got dressed.

"Hey!" Sid yelled. "Don't be sore!"

They all scrambled out of the water and ran over to him.

"We were just joking around with you!"

"We didn't mean to scare you so bad."

"We always do pranks!"

But Chet wasn't listening. His heart was pounding and his cheeks burned. He laced up his boots, stood up, and stormed away.

CHAPTER 6

The next day the guys came by the diner, smiling like everything was normal. Chet didn't wave back. He slipped into the kitchen before they sat down at the counter and didn't come out until they were gone.

After the breakfast rush was over, Uncle Jerry handed Chet a mug of root beer and told him to have a seat.

"What's wrong, kiddo?" he asked, sitting

on the stool next to Chet's. "I see you've been avoiding your buddies."

"They're not my buddies," Chet said. "I hardly know them."

Uncle Jerry peered at Chet. "Is this because of that stunt at the creek?"

"You heard about that?" Chet said.

Uncle Jerry chuckled, but not in a nasty way. "They didn't mean any harm," he said. "You should be flattered."

"How's that?" Chet said. "They made me feel like an idiot."

"It means they like you, that you're one of them," Uncle Jerry said. "Now they're expecting you to get them back. Didn't you know that's how it works?"

How could Chet know? He'd never had any real friends before. He wanted to know more. But before he could ask, Mr. Colton and Dr. Jay came through the door. They were Uncle

Jerry's oldest friends. Mr. Colton owned the hardware store. Dr. Jay took care of practically everyone in town. They came in every day for coffee and to chat about baseball with Uncle Jerry.

But today the men didn't want to talk about Babe Ruth's pitching record. Mr. Colton held up the morning paper so Uncle Jerry and Chet could read the front-page headline.

SHARK KILLS SECOND BATHER IN NEW JERSEY

July 7, 1916
Spring Lake, New Jersey

A shark attacked Charles Bruder, 28, while he was swimming alone in the ocean yesterday afternoon. Lifeguards rushed to his rescue, but the young man's wounds were so severe that he bled to death before they reached shore.

Bruder, a well-liked bell captain at the Essex

and Sussex Hotel, was known to be a strong swimmer. But he was no match for the beast, which attacked without mercy. Before he perished, Bruder was able to tell a remarkable story to his rescuers.

"He was a big gray fellow, and as rough as sandpaper," Bruder said. "I didn't see him until after he struck me the first time. . . . That was when I yelled. . . . I thought he had gone on, but he only turned and shot back at me [and] . . . snipped my left leg off. . . . He yanked me clear under before he let go. . . . He came back at me . . . and he shook me like a terrier shakes a rat."

Bruder tried to say more, but he became too weak. He died of massive blood loss and shock before lifeguards could get him back to the shore.

Officials are warning people not to swim alone.

"I still don't believe it," said Uncle Jerry. "Someone is cooking up these stories to sell newspapers."

"Could be," Mr. Colton said. "Folks are terrified, though. My wife's cousin lives out there, and she says nobody will go near the ocean. They have fishermen out with rifles shooting at anything that moves."

"You know what this reminds me of?" Dr. Jay said. "The Creek Devil."

"What's that?" Chet asked.

Mr. Colton and Dr. Jay chuckled. Then Mr. Colton shifted his hefty body forward on the stool. He leaned closer to Chet.

"Old-timers say there's a monster that lives down near the creek. He's covered with mud. Eats snakes and bats and makes a terrible hissing sound. Moans, too. Legend is that he comes out every decade and drags a kid back into the mud with him."

"People believe that?" Chet said.

"Everyone in town knows the legend," Uncle Jerry said, "but nobody really believes it."

"Except for Jerry here," Dr. Jay said, slapping Uncle Jerry on the shoulder. "When we were little, he wouldn't go near that creek!"

"Bah," Uncle Jerry said, waving his hand at Dr. Jay. "I don't know what you're talking about. Doesn't someone need a wart removed or something?"

Was Uncle Jerry blushing?

Imagine Uncle Jerry being afraid of a made-up monster! Chet smiled to himself. Maybe there was hope for him yet.

Suddenly Chet had an idea for the greatest prank ever. Folks would be talking about it for years. And then he'd be part of the gang for sure.

Dewey, Monty, and Sid were going to come face-to-face with the Creek Devil.

CHAPTER 7

At church on Sunday, Chet went out of his way to say hi to the guys. They seemed relieved that he wasn't mad anymore. And the truth was, he really wasn't, now that he understood how it was with pranks—and now that he had a genius plan for getting them back.

"Come swimming with us today," Sid called as he helped his mother into their buggy. "We'll be there right after lunch."

"Sure!" Chet called back. "I'll meet you!"

Uncle Jerry patted him on the back.

"That's the way, kiddo," he said. "There's no room in a small town for grudges."

Chet was dying to tell Uncle Jerry about his idea. But Chet kept his mouth shut, worried that his uncle might tell someone and spoil the plan.

He saw Minnie Marston as he was leaving the churchyard. She waved to him and smiled, like she wanted him to go up and talk to her. For months last spring Chet had prayed that Minnie would look in his direction. But now? He didn't have time for girls, not even Minnie. He had to get to the creek before the guys. He waved to Minnie and headed home.

Uncle Jerry was going to the diner to take care of some bookkeeping, and Chet headed home to change. He grabbed the bag he'd packed that morning. Inside was a bottle of ketchup, one of his old work boots, and the white cap he always wore at work — everything he needed.

He hurried to the creek, which was completely quiet, and went straight to work.

His plan had two parts. First, he wanted to make the guys think he'd been attacked and dragged, bloody and screaming, into the creek. He dribbled some ketchup along the dock — a trail of blood. He put his boot in the middle of the dock and covered it with ketchup. He did the same to his cap.

Chet stood back and admired his work.

So far, so good.

Now Chet took off his undershirt and trousers and kicked off his boots. He hid them in the tall grass. Then he went to the wettest part of the bank. He scooped up handfuls of the slimiest mud he could find and smeared it onto his face, his arms, and his chest. He used extra mud to cover his head so that no hairs poked through. He had no idea what the Creek Devil was supposed to look like, but he was pretty sure it didn't have orange hair.

Chet was just finishing when he heard voices. The guys!

Chet closed his eyes and took a deep breath.

Then he let out the biggest, loudest scream he could muster. He screamed like he was terrified, like he was in agony. And then he splashed loudly into the creek, careful not to wash off the mud. He screamed some more, and then waded into the reeds and hid.

"Chet?" Sid called. "That you?"

Chet didn't answer. He couldn't see the guys, but he heard their heavy breathing and their panicky voices.

"Where is he?"

"Is that his boot?"

"What the . . ."

"Oh, my God," Sid whispered. "Is that blood?"

Chet held his breath. Would they really fall for it? Could this actually work?

"Chet?" Sid called. "Chet, you there?"

Chet had to puff up his cheeks to keep from bursting out laughing.

"Isn't that Chet's cap?" Dewey whispered.

A few seconds went by.

"What's happening?" Monty said quietly.

They were falling for it! Now it was time for part two.

Chet gave a low hiss, remembering what Mr. Colton had said about the sound the Creek Devil made before an attack.

"What the heck was that?" Dewey said, his voice shaking.

"Quiet!" Sid said.

"Should we go get someone?" Dewey said.

"HISSSSSSSSSSSSSSSSSS."

Chet was impressed by how spooky he sounded. Next he started to moan, low at first, and then louder.

"OOOOOOMMMMMMMOOOOOO."

He poked his head through the reeds, not all the way through, just enough for the guys to

catch a glimpse of a hideous head covered with black slime.

The guys stared with bugged-out eyes and wide-open mouths.

"Ahhhhhhhh!" they screamed.

Dewey went tearing away.

"OOOOOOMMMMMMMOOOOOO!"

"AHHHHHHHHHH!" screamed Sid and Monty.

They turned to run, and that's when Chet leaped out of the water.

"Got you!" Chet shouted.

Sid and Monty stopped short. Their faces were dead white.

"I got you good!"

He waited for their terrified faces to melt into smiles, for them to laugh their heads off and tell Chet he was a genius.

But they didn't.

Sid stomped onto the dock. He leaned close

to Chet, his face all twisted up and furious. His fists were clenched.

Chet jumped back. Was Sid going to deck him?

Monty pulled him away. "He's not worth it," he said.

"You're an *idiot*!" Sid growled. "We really thought something bad happened to you!"

"How could you think that would be *funny*?" Monty said.

The words came at him hard and cold.

Sid glared at him a few more seconds. And then they turned and walked away.

Chet stood there in shock.

His prank had worked better than he could have imagined.

But it was all wrong.

And here he was, covered with stinking mud, all alone.

CHAPTER 8

Chet scrubbed himself off in the creek and went back to Uncle Jerry's cottage.

It was too hot to be inside, so he sat on the porch. He sat there a long time. He wondered what Mama and Papa were doing. He pictured Mama, with her soft smile and laughing eyes. And Papa, who always woke up with a happy face, even when they were out of money and had to pack up to start all over again.

Why had they left him here?

He was so deep in his gloomy thoughts that at first he didn't see Uncle Jerry hurrying up the walk.

"There you are!" he said, catching his breath. He sat down next to Chet.

"I thought you were going to be at the diner all day," Chet said.

"I was," Uncle Jerry said, fishing in his pocket for his pipe. He struck his match on the floor, lit the pipe, took a few puffs, and then settled back.

They didn't say anything for a few minutes.

"So there was some excitement at the creek, I hear," Uncle Jerry said.

Chet's heart sank into his boots.

"Poor Dewey came running down Main Street in his drawers," Uncle Jerry continued. "He was screaming about the Creek Devil. His mama called Dr. Jay."

Chet sighed. He didn't look at Uncle Jerry. He'd probably already sent a telegram to Mama and Papa, and was getting ready to ship Chet directly to California. Chet couldn't wait to start packing.

"I went too far," Chet said.

"I guess you did," Uncle Jerry said.

Chet took a deep breath. A spider scurried across the floor and disappeared into one of the cracks. Lucky spider.

There was a strange sound. Chet looked at Uncle Jerry, whose face was beet red. Was he choking on his pipe smoke?

No. He was laughing! His laughter exploded through the air. He pounded his chest a few times. "Sorry," he said through his guffaws. "But that look on Dewey's face . . ." He leaned forward, slapping his leg, shaking his head. "It was a good one," Uncle Jerry sputtered. "Maybe a little too gruesome. But darned good."

Chet wanted to laugh along with Uncle Jerry. But he kept thinking of that furious look on Sid's face when Chet came out of the water.

Monty was right. Chet wasn't worth it. He wasn't even worth a punch in the nose. He had ruined everything!

Tears ran down his face. He turned away from Uncle Jerry, but it was too late.

Uncle Jerry stopped laughing and put his hand on Chet's shoulder. He waited for Chet to stop crying.

What a fool he was, blubbering like this! Over a stupid prank.

"It's all right," Uncle Jerry said.

"No," Chet said, standing up. "I need to leave."

"Where are you going?" Uncle Jerry said.

"To California," Chet said.

Uncle Jerry stared at him.

"I don't belong here," Chet said.

"The heck you don't!" Uncle Jerry said. "You belong here. Like I knew you would. Why do you think I begged your mama to let you stay with me?"

"But I thought Mama asked *you*," Chet said.

"Are you kidding? I've been begging for years. I wrote about a hundred letters, a few telegrams too."

"Why?" Chet said.

Uncle Jerry looked at Chet like he'd asked for the answer to two plus two.

"I thought maybe you were tired of moving around so much," Uncle Jerry said, pulling Chet back down to sit next to him on the porch step. "And there's another reason. You and I are buddies, kiddo. Always were. I was lonely without you all these years."

Chet almost laughed. With all the people who loved Uncle Jerry, who crowded around him every day at the diner, who laughed at his jokes and listened to his stories, how could he be lonely?

Yet Uncle Jerry's eyes, usually all crinkled up and merry, were big and serious. He meant it.

"Did I ever tell you what happened after I hurt my leg?" Uncle Jerry said. "I moved to New

York City. I quit this town. I just wanted to get lost. I couldn't stand the way people looked at me here, like they pitied me. Or like I'd let them down by not becoming a big baseball star."

"Mama never told me that," Chet said.

"Well it's true. But you know what? I missed this place. And I'll tell you what I learned: A person has to face up to things. You never solve anything by running away."

Chet knew Uncle Jerry was right. But how could Chet stay here with the guys hating him so much?

Uncle Jerry seemed to read his thoughts. "You'll find a way to make it up to those friends of yours," he said. "I know you will."

CHAPTER 9

The next two days at the diner, Chet kept waiting for the guys to come in. Every time the door opened, he looked up, hoping to see them elbowing each other to be first to the counter.

They never even walked by.

Chet kept trying to work up the nerve to go and find them, and finally on Wednesday he was ready. It was another scorching day, the hottest yet. After the lunch rush was over, Uncle

Jerry decided to close the diner early. All the ice in the restaurant had melted. The milk had curdled. You could just about cook a flapjack on the kitchen floor.

"I'm going home to stick my head under the water pump," Uncle Jerry said. "Then I'm going to swing in our hammock until the sun sets."

Chet said good-bye to Uncle Jerry and headed for the creek, sure he'd find the guys playing ball in the water.

But the swimming hole was quiet.

Chet realized they were still at the factory. Their shift wouldn't be over for an hour.

While he was waiting, he noticed that there were still splotches of ketchup on the dock. They looked even more like blood now, like evidence of a gruesome crime. He decided to try to clean them before the guys got here, to erase all reminders of his prank. He undressed and jumped into the creek. Then he splashed water up onto the dock, hopped out of the water, and scrubbed the stains with a handful of leaves.

It took three rounds of splashing and scrubbing to clean it up.

By then Chet was so hot that he decided to take a longer swim.

It was peaceful here without everyone splashing and shouting. He floated on his back under the trees, remembering how Papa had taught him to swim in the Mississippi, how Mama sat on the banks waving and clapping.

He had turned to swim back to the dock when — *crash*, he hit something under the water.

Or something hit him.

Hit him so hard in the chest he couldn't breathe.

What was that? An old dock plank? A snapping turtle? Had Sid sneaked up on him and smacked him?

The water around him looked funny, like it was filled with red smoke.

Chet looked down in shock. His entire chest was scraped and oozing blood. What could have done that to him?

A cold terror rose up inside him. He suddenly had the feeling that someone — or something — was nearby, watching him.

And then he saw it.

A gray fin.

It glistened in the bright sun as it glided slowly toward him.

He had to be seeing things. Or could this be another prank? Were the guys getting him back?

But no, this was no tile.

As it got closer, Chet could see the dark shape of an enormous fish, bigger than him. Even bigger than Uncle Jerry. Two black eyes peered up through the water.

Chet's heart stopped.

Killer eyes.

Chet took off toward the shore, pounding through the water, kicking with all his might. Finally his feet touched the bottom. He was running now, his heart hammering, a voice booming through his mind. *Get out of the water! Get out of the water! Get out of the water!*

Almost there — just a few more steps!

He dove forward, landing hard in the dirt. He rolled onto his side and stared in disbelief: It was a shark, a massive shark — dirty gray on top and pure white underneath. Its jaws snapped open and closed. The teeth, jagged and needle sharp, were bigger than Chet's fingers, lined up in rows and curving inward. The shark thrashed, as if it was trying to push itself up onto the bank. Chet wanted to get up and run. But he was frozen to the ground.

Those killer eyes stared unblinkingly at Chet.

And then, with a flick of its tail, the shark thrust itself backward into the water.

It hovered for a second on the surface.

Then, with a *whoosh* of its tail, it disappeared back down the creek.

CHAPTER 10

Chet rose to his knees and threw up.

When he could stand, he staggered over to his clothes. His hands were shaking so badly that he could barely button his shirt. He shoved his feet into his boots, not even trying to lace them. And then on wobbly legs, his blood pounding in his ears, he ran up the hill and found his way to Main Street.

He pushed past the ladies with their shopping baskets. He crossed the street, ignoring the honking motorcar that swerved around him. A man in a buggy shouted at him to watch out. The horse whinnied. Chet barely noticed.

He staggered into Mr. Colton's hardware store, tripping across the doorway and knocking over a display of watering cans. The clattering brought three customers to the front of the store. Mr. Colton hurried out from behind the counter.

"Chet?" he said worriedly. "What's wrong?"

Chet opened his mouth.

But he couldn't speak.

"What happened?" Mr. Colton said. "Why is your shirt covered with blood? Are you bleeding? Who did this to you?"

A small group of customers clustered around him, their eyes filled with concern.

Finally, Chet got the words out. "A shark."

"What?" Mr. Colton said.

"A shark," Chet repeated.

"Has there been another attack on the shore?"

Mr. Colton said. "I didn't see anything in the newspaper."

Chet shook his head.

"There's a shark in the creek," he said. "I saw it. It crashed into me."

The crowd erupted into loud laughter.

Mr. Colton offered a sympathetic smile and a hand on his shoulder. "It's the heat, my boy. It's driving us all a little mad."

He asked one of the customers to go into the back and bring Chet a drink. He led Chet through the laughing crowd and sat him on the stool behind the counter. A man handed Chet a tin mug of water.

"Take a drink, son," Mr. Colton said. But Chet pushed it away, and water splashed onto a pile of seed catalogs.

"We have to warn people!"

But Mr. Colton just shook his head, like Chet was a little kid who was sure he'd seen a unicorn galloping down the sidewalk.

"There's so much garbage floating in that creek," Mr. Colton said. "It could have been a plank from the dock, or a barrel, or a—"

"No," Chet said. "It was a shark!"

"I think maybe all those pranks are getting to you," Mr. Colton said.

Chet knew that he must sound crazy, that he could spend all day swearing that he'd seen a shark. Nobody would believe him.

Why would they?

A shark in the creek? It was impossible!

Except that Chet had seen it with his own eyes. If he'd been a step slower, he'd be dead right now, another name in the newspaper.

"It's all right, son," Mr. Colton said. "How about I call Dr. Jay and he'll give you a ride home. You've never been in his motorcar, have you?"

Mr. Colton headed to the back of the store to use the telephone.

The customers drifted away, shaking their heads and chuckling.

No, nobody would believe it. Meanwhile, that shark was still in the creek.

And then it hit Chet . . . that there was one person in town who just might believe him, who might know what to do. He wasn't sure, but it was his best hope.

He slid off the stool and rushed out of the store.

"Chet!" Mr. Colton called. "Where are you going?"

Chet didn't turn around.

He had to find Captain Wilson. He'd wasted enough time already.

CHAPTER 11

Chet stood on the sagging porch of the Captain's house. He'd barely knocked when the front door swung open.

The Captain stood there with a scowl on his crumpled-up face.

He looked at Chet like he'd never seen him before.

"Yes?" he said. "What is this about?"

Chet's heart sank.

He thought of what Uncle Jerry had said, that the Captain's mind was like Swiss cheese, full of holes and gaps in his memory.

"What is it?" the Captain said. "Are you selling something? I don't have all day."

"Sorry, sir," Chet said. "I didn't mean to bother you."

He almost turned around and walked away. But he forced himself to stay put. He stepped forward, close to the Captain, and peered right into his eyes.

"Captain," he said in a loud voice. "I saw a shark. In the creek. It crashed into me."

Chet lifted his shirt to show the angry-looking scrape.

The Captain stared at Chet's chest. Then he looked into the distance. Did he even know where he was?

"I know it sounds impossible, sir. It doesn't make any sense at all."

The Captain looked back at Chet. "Sure it does," he said.

Chet's eyes widened in surprise.

"The creek empties out into the Raritan Bay, which leads right to the Atlantic. Pirates used to come to these parts. Buried their treasure all around here."

The Captain's eyes kept getting brighter.

"If the tides are high, and the currents are strong, a shark could get swept right up into the creek."

Of course it could.

"I saw it, Captain," Chet said, more confident now. "It was huge. And its eyes, just like you said . . ."

"Killer eyes," the Captain muttered.

Chet nodded.

"Why are you standing here, son?" the Captain scolded. "We need to warn people! I'm getting my boat. You get down to that swimming hole. You tell people what you saw."

"What if they won't believe me?" Chet asked.

The Captain put a hand on Chet's shoulder. His grip was very strong.

"Go!" he said.

CHAPTER 12

Chet started shouting halfway down the big hill. "Get out of the water!" he screamed. "Get out! Get out now!"

He thundered down the path and onto the dock. "You have to get out! There's a shark!"

The guys were all there—but they didn't even look at Chet.

"You have to believe me!" Chet insisted. "This isn't a joke. You have to get out!"

"You hear that, Monty?" Sid said. "There's a shark in the creek! We better get out."

Sid hoisted himself up onto the dock, and Monty and Dewey followed.

Was it working? Were they listening?

But then Sid backed up and took a running leap off the edge of the dock. He cannonballed into the creek with such an enormous splash that Chet got drenched. Monty and Dewey dove in after him.

"Hey," Sid called. "If the shark attacks me, you guys can split the five-hundred-buck reward from that rich guy."

"That guy's dead!" Monty said.

"Too bad!" said Sid.

"Oh, shaaaaaaa-rrrrrrrk!" Monty called through cupped hands. "Here, sharky shark! Come and get us!"

They hooted with laughter, and Chet stood there, totally helpless. That shark was probably long gone. Nobody would ever believe him. For the next hundred years, people around Elm Hills would be talking about Chet Roscow, the kid who had said there was a shark in the creek. He'd be a big joke, like the Captain was.

Chet felt like running away, far away. All the way to California.

But then he noticed Sid, strangely still in the creek. His face had gone white. His mouth was open, like he was going to scream.

Chet's insides turned to jelly when he saw the glistening fin moving slowly through the water.

"What the . . ." Dewey said.

"Hurry!" Chet cried. "Get out!"

Monty and Dewey flew out of the water.

But Sid seemed stuck, hypnotized.

The shark was closer to the surface now, its black eyes almost glowing. Its massive body looming.

They all screamed at Sid.

"Get out!"

"Hurry!"

"Come on! It's coming!"

Chet heard a motor in the distance, and Captain's Wilson's voice shouting, *"Shark! Shark in the creek! Everyone out! Shark in the creek!"*

Sid still didn't budge.

The shark was getting closer.

Suddenly, before he had a chance to think, Chet was in the water, swimming as fast as he

could toward Sid. He grabbed hold of Sid's arm and pulled him.

"Chet! Is it real?" Sid gasped. "Is it real?"

"Yes, yes, hurry!"

Monty and Dewey were at the edge of the dock, reaching down for them. Sid hoisted himself up, and Chet planted his hands on the dock. The guys all grabbed his arms to pull him up. Chet was almost out of the water when something caught his leg.

At first it felt like a giant hand was grabbing him. Then it felt like hot nails were boring into his calf.

"It's got my leg!" Chet screamed.

"Pull!" Sid shouted.

His friends pulled. They pulled and pulled until Chet was sure he'd be torn in two. After an eternity, his leg finally came free!

His friends hauled him onto the dock.

But then the shark exploded out of the water, its jaws wide open, its teeth smeared with blood. Its gaping mouth was coming right for Chet. And then —

BANG!

A gunshot shattered the air.

Time seemed to stop.

The next thing Chet knew, he was sitting on the dock. Everything looked foggy, and people seemed to be moving in slow motion. He heard muffled noises — men's voices, a boat's motor.

And the guys, saying his name over and over.

They were leaning close, still holding tight to his arms.

Chet looked down and wondered what he was doing in a puddle of ketchup. Hadn't he cleaned that up? Why was the puddle getting bigger?

Chet realized it wasn't the ketchup. It was blood pouring from his leg.

The fog around him grew thicker, until Chet couldn't see or hear a thing.

CHAPTER 13

SHARK KILLS TWO IN NEW JERSEY CREEK
A third boy survives, but injuries are grave

JULY 13, 1916

ELM HILLS, NEW JERSEY

A boy and a young man were killed yesterday, July 12, by a monster shark that made a shocking appearance in the Matawan Creek in New Jersey. Lester Stillwell, 11, was killed while swimming with friends in the town of Matawan. Minutes later, Stanley Fisher, 24, was killed as he bravely attempted to rescue young Lester.

Farther up the creek, Chet Roscow, 10, encountered the shark as he swam by himself. He managed to escape, and ran into town to alert residents. His cries of warning were ignored, with most residents dismissing his story as a prank. The boy did not give up, and later attempted to warn his friends, who were swimming behind the Templer Tile Factory. It was during these efforts that the lad fell into the jaws of the monstrous shark.

He was rescued moments later when Captain Thomas A. Wilson shot at the shark with a Civil War musket, scaring the beast away.

The brave youth was rushed to St. Peter's Hospital in New Brunswick. Injuries to his leg are described as extremely grave.

CHAPTER 14

Pictures floated in and out of Chet's mind. Fuzzy pictures — men lifting him off the dock, the inside of Dr. Jay's motorcar, the white walls and white sheets of the hospital, unsmiling doctors shaking their heads, a pretty nurse with a soft voice. And Uncle Jerry, who always seemed to be sitting right next to Chet.

Was Chet asleep? Was he awake? Was he alive or was he dead?

It was two days before Chet decided for sure he was alive, and three more before he understood what had happened to him — that the shark had ripped away part of his calf. Another few seconds and that shark would have taken off his whole leg.

"It will heal," the doctor said, patting Chet on the shoulder. "It will take some time. But your leg will heal."

"The miracle kid," said Uncle Jerry. "That's what the newspapers are calling you. And it's true."

By then Chet had heard about the others — the boy attacked a mile down the creek from Elm Hills and the man who jumped in to try to save him. Both were dead.

Chet's room was filled with flowers and cards from people all over the country.

But none of it mattered to him. His leg hurt worse than it had when the shark was biting

him. The medicine they gave him made him feel sick and woozy. He wanted Mama and Papa, but their train was still making its way across the country.

Every time Chet fell asleep, he woke up suddenly, shaking with fear, his bed soaked with sweat. The terror faded some when he was awake. But somehow that shark was always lurking. Its black killer eyes watching him, its bloody teeth glistening.

Chet had never felt so alone.

CHAPTER 15

It was Chet's sixth morning in the hospital when there was a knock at his door. He sat up, sure it was Mama and Papa.

But it wasn't. Dewey, Sid, and Monty stood in the doorway. Uncle Jerry was right behind them. The hospital was a two-hour trip from Elm Hills. Had the guys really come all this way to see him?

They all looked a little scared, and Chet felt nervous. Were they still mad at him? Chet raised

his hand and gave the briefest, tiniest wave. And just like that, the guys came barreling across the room, fighting each other for a spot on his little bed. Their jostling hurt his leg, but Chet couldn't have cared less.

"I'll be in the hallway, kiddo," Uncle Jerry said. "I think that pretty nurse likes me."

The door closed, and all the guys started talking at once.

"They dynamited the creek!"

"A guy caught a shark in the bay, says it's the same shark!"

"It was ten feet long!"

"They cut open its stomach."

"They found human bones!"

Of course Uncle Jerry had told Chet all this. But he didn't stop the guys from telling him again. He liked the sound of their voices around him. He hoped they never stopped talking. They told him that Captain Wilson was a celebrity, that newspaper reporters were coming from around the world to talk to him.

"Your uncle said your leg will be okay," Dewey said.

"You're going to have a huge scar," Sid said. He sounded almost jealous.

Chet hadn't looked too closely at his leg when the nurses changed his bandages. That was when it hurt the most, when they washed the wound. He had to keep his eyes closed tight and bite down on a rag to keep from screaming until the cleaning was done. A chunk of flesh was missing from his calf. He'd have more than a scar. He'd have a limp.

"Just like me," Uncle Jerry had said. "Won't slow you down a bit."

"Minnie keeps asking about you," Dewey said.

Chet wondered what Minnie would think of a boy with a limp.

Sid moved a little closer to Chet. "We're sorry," he whispered.

"We're sorry for everything," said Monty.

Sid looked like he was about to cry. "It's my fault."

"What?" Chet said. "You didn't put the shark in the creek."

Sid laughed a little, and wiped his eyes on his sleeve.

"We should have listened to you," Monty said. "If we had gotten out of the water, you wouldn't have gotten bitten."

"And if you hadn't come," Dewey said, "we'd be . . ."

"But if I hadn't played that stupid prank," Chet said, "you would have believed me."

"You saved me," Sid said.

"You guys saved *me*," Chet said. He swallowed hard, and they all sniffled a little.

Then a hush came over the room. And in that quiet moment, Chet realized something: He and the guys would always be tied together. By the terrible things they'd seen. By what they'd done for each other.

It was a while before Sid said, "We're calling a truce. No more pranks."

As usual, nobody argued with Sid. It was settled.

The guys stayed all afternoon, until Uncle Jerry poked his head in and said it was time to go. The guys lingered until Uncle Jerry shooed them out the door.

"Wait for me," Uncle Jerry told them, and then he closed the door and came over to Chet's bed.

"Your mama called the hospital," he said. "She and your papa will be here after dinner tonight."

Chet smiled.

"You know," Uncle Jerry said, straightening the sheet, "I had an idea, thought I'd mention it to you."

He cleared his throat.

"Maybe your papa would like to help me run the diner," Uncle Jerry said. "It's a busy place. I think he might enjoy it. We do well enough. And I sure wouldn't mind having more time to myself."

It took Chet a few seconds to understand what Uncle Jerry was saying.

"Your papa might decide it's time to settle

down," Uncle Jerry said. "I'm not sure he'll say yes, but I guess it's worth a try, don't you think?"

Chet opened his mouth to say something, but the words seemed to be all stuck together. So he just nodded.

"Okay then, kiddo. It's a plan."

Chet lay there a while after Uncle Jerry left. He thought about Mama and Papa. He couldn't wait to introduce them to the guys, and to Captain Wilson. He struggled to keep his eyes open, but it had been a long day. Before long he dozed off.

He dreamed that he was an old man, sitting in a diner, telling a story to a gang of boys. He told them about a shark in a creek, a huge killer shark with bloody jaws and coal-black eyes. He described how the shark had chased him, how it scared him out of his wits. But in the end, the beast couldn't get him. Because Chet hadn't been alone. Because his friends had reached out for him. They'd held him tight.

And they never let him go.

THE SHARK ATTACKS OF 1916: AN UNBELIEVABLE TRUE STORY

Imagine reading an article about a rabbit that suddenly turned into a bloodthirsty killer.

You would laugh, maybe, or shake your head in disbelief.

That's how most Americans in 1916 felt when they first heard about the shark attacks along the New Jersey shore. A shark attacking a human? Impossible! Sharks are tame creatures, most people believed, easily scared, with jaws too weak to do real damage to a human. There were no real marine biologists in those days, no scuba gear or submarines for underwater exploration. There had never been close studies of sharks, just stories passed down over generations. And of course everyone knew about Hermann Oelrichs and his famous reward: In 1891, the tycoon had offered $500 to anyone who could prove that a person had ever been attacked by a shark along the East Coast of the United States, north of North Carolina. Decades went by and nobody collected the reward. This seemed to confirm the popular belief that sharks posed no danger to humans.

And then came the attacks of 1916.

Though the characters in my book are made up, the major events of the story are true. Over twelve days during the scorching hot July of 1916, four people were killed in shark attacks. First Charles Vansant and then Charles Bruder were fatally wounded swimming in the ocean. Then, sixteen miles from the ocean, eleven-year-old Lester Stillwell was killed while he was swimming with his buddies in the Matawan Creek. Twenty-four-year-old Stanley Fisher was attacked trying to rescue Lester. Twelve-year-old Joseph Dunn was bitten on the leg but survived, just like Chet.

These attacks shocked America and shattered false ideas about sharks. There was no doubt that these were shark attacks. Two days after the Matawan attacks, a great white shark was caught in the Raritan Bay. It had human bones in its stomach, which seemed to prove that the killer had been caught.

But over the past few decades, scientists and investigators have raised questions about the attacks. Many doubt a lone great white was responsible. They say a bull shark is more likely to have attacked in the Matawan Creek, since that is the only man-eating species that can easily survive in fresh water for a length of time. In the weeks before the first attacks, ship captains had reported seeing more sharks than usual in the Atlantic shipping lanes, including great whites and bull sharks. Perhaps some unusual ocean or weather conditions had attracted sharks to the shore areas, where they tragically crossed paths with swimmers. We will never know for sure.

What we do know is that shark attacks are extremely rare.

And that the attacks of 1916 will never be forgotten.

Lauren Tarshis

FACTS ABOUT
SHARK ATTACKS

- Of the more than 350 known species of sharks, only 4 are particularly prone to attack a human: the bull shark, the great white, the tiger shark, and the hammerhead. The bull shark is considered by many experts to be the most dangerous to humans.

- Shark attacks are very rare. In 2008, there were 118 attacks reported world-wide, and 4 deaths. Of those attacks, 59 were "unprovoked," which means that the shark attacked someone who was not doing anything to deliberately at-tract or touch it. In contrast, an av-erage of 125,000 people die of snake-bites each year.

- Some scientists believe that most sharks don't mean to attack humans, but mistake surfers or swimmers for large sea mammals, like seals. This could explain why most shark attacks on humans are not fatal — a shark takes one bite, realizes its mistake, and swims away.

- Most shark attacks happen to people swimming alone in the ocean. Experts suggest that the best way to avoid an attack is to swim in groups. Other tips: Avoid swimming at night or at dusk. Swimming with a dog can be dangerous, because the whirling motion of the dog's paws in the water can attract sharks. Leave jewelry at home, since bright objects can also attract sharks. And don't swim in the ocean if you have a bleeding wound.

- Florida is the number-one shark-attack state, with an average of thirty attacks a year. There have been no deaths over the past four years. California, Hawaii, North Carolina, and South Carolina have had a few attacks over the last five years. There has not been another attack recorded in New Jersey since 1926.

- Every year, humans kill nearly 100 million sharks, mainly for their fins, which are a prized ingredient for shark fin soup. Many shark species are endangered, including the great white.

- The International Shark Attack File investigates every reported shark attack in the world and maintains detailed records. Check out their fascinating website: http://www.flmnh.ufl.edu/fish/

THE NEW YORK TIMES BESTSELLING SERIES
I SURVIVED
HURRICANE KATRINA, 2005
by Lauren Tarshis
SCHOLASTIC

I SURVIVED

HURRICANE
KATRINA, 2005

by Lauren Tarshis

illustrated by Scott Dawson

Scholastic Inc.

CHAPTER 1

MONDAY, AUGUST 29, 2005
7:00 A.M.
THE LOWER NINTH WARD,
NEW ORLEANS, LOUISIANA

Hurricane Katrina was ripping apart New Orleans, and eleven-year-old Barry Tucker was lost and alone, clinging to an oak tree for dear life. He'd fallen off the roof of his house and been swept away in the floodwater. The raging current

209

had tossed and twisted him, almost tearing him to pieces. He would have drowned, but somehow Barry had grabbed hold of the tree. With every bit of strength in his body, he'd pulled himself out of the water and wrapped his arms and legs around the trunk.

Now he was holding on, with no idea what to do next.

Wind howled around him. Rain hammered down. And all Barry could see was water. Swirling, foaming, rushing water. The water had washed away his whole neighborhood. Pieces of it floated by. In the dirty gray light, Barry saw jagged hunks of wood, shattered glass, a twisted bicycle, a refrigerator, a stuffed penguin, a mattress covered with a pink blanket. He tried hard not to imagine what else was in that water or what had happened to all his neighbors . . . and his mom and dad and little sister, Cleo.

What if they'd all fallen into the water too? What if . . .

Wait! What was that sound? Was someone calling his name?

"Dad!" Barry screamed. "Mom! Cleo!"

No. It was just the wind shrieking. Even the sky was terrified of this storm.

Barry was shaking now. Tears stung his eyes. And then he heard a new sound, a cracking and groaning, above the wind and rain. He stared in shock at what was floating in the water.

A house.

Or what was left of it. One side was torn off. It moved through the flood slowly, turning. Its blown-out windows seemed to stare at Barry. The splintered wood looked like teeth in a wide-open mouth.

And it was coming right at him.

CHAPTER 2

TWENTY-ONE HOURS EARLIER
SUNDAY, AUGUST 28, 2005
10:00 A.M.
THE TUCKERS' HOUSE,
THE LOWER NINTH WARD,
NEW ORLEANS, LOUISIANA

Barry sat on the steps of his front porch. His best friend, Jay, huddled next to him. Jay wanted to see the drawing rolled up in Barry's hands.

"Show me!" Jay said, leaning so close Barry could smell egg sandwich on his breath.

Barry elbowed him back, laughing. He knew Jay was excited. They both were.

The next day was the deadline for Acclaim Comic Books' "Create a Superhero" contest. For the past three weeks, Barry and Jay had been working nonstop on their creation. They'd come up with everything together — their hero's name, his costume, even his secret star, which was the source of his amazing powers. But it had been Barry's job to draw him. He'd stayed up past midnight the last three nights, adding his finishing touches.

"Okay," Barry said, clearing his throat and standing up like an announcer facing an anxious crowd. "This is the moment you've been waiting for. Ladies and gentlemen, meet Akivo!"

He unrolled the paper and watched Jay's eyes get wider behind his scratched-up glasses.

Barry's cheeks heated up. He'd worked hard

on the drawing. Of course he'd never admit it to Jay, but it was almost like Akivo was his brother. A seven-foot-tall brother with bulging muscles, hawk wings, titanium armor, and eyes that could see through walls.

Jay rose to his feet. "That's amazing," he said in a shocked whisper. "The wings look real. And that fire . . ." He pointed to the flames coming out of Akivo's silver boots. Barry had worked for three hours on those flames, mixing orange and red and yellow with a bit of blue until they looked like they would burn your fingers if you touched them.

They both stood there for a minute, staring at the drawing.

Then Jay started jumping up and down.

"We're going to win the contest!" Jay yelled. "We're going to win the contest!"

Barry started jumping too. He knew that hundreds of people were entering, and not only kids. Some people drew on computers. Others

made videos. All Barry had were the colored pencils Mom and Dad had bought him for his last birthday.

Still, Barry was a believer. He had gotten that from his mom. And at that minute, Barry let himself believe that he and Jay just might win first place — $250 to split and the comic book, starring Akivo, that Acclaim would create. Barry and Jay loved comic books. They'd been collecting them since they'd learned to read.

"We're going to be rich!" Jay sang.

"And famous!" said Barry.

They were so busy jumping and dancing and hooting, they didn't notice Abe Mackay and his killer dog, Cruz, watching from the sidewalk. Abe's laughter got their attention. Abe was a huge guy — almost twice the size of Barry. His booming laugh practically shook the ground.

Barry and Jay froze. The hairs on Barry's arms stood up straight. Jay's cocoa skin turned gray.

Abe was in middle school, just a year older

than Barry and Jay. They used to all be friends. But Abe had changed since his dad had gone away two years earlier. Now he and his grandma lived alone. The Mackays' house used to be one of the nicest in their neighborhood. It was painted bright sky blue. Abe's grandma used to have a yard full of flowers you could smell a block away. But now the garden was dead and the house was gloomy. Abe didn't go to school much anymore, and he'd started hanging around the older boys whose *vroom*ing motorcycles kept everyone up at night.

And then there was his new dog. He looked like a big mutt. He had a square head, and the tips of his pointy ears flopped over. But Abe said that he was a special breed from Asia, trained by the Chinese army, and that his jaw was strong enough to bite through metal. "He's trained to kill," Abe had bragged. "On my command. He goes right for the neck. One bite is all it takes."

"Why'd you stop dancing?" Abe asked now, spitting onto the sidewalk. "Cruz loves to dance!"

He bent down to unhook the dog's leash.

"Go!" Abe shouted. "Go get 'em, Cruz!"

CHAPTER 3

Barry turned and put his hands over his face, bracing for the feeling of teeth ripping at his neck. But nothing happened.

He peeled open his eyes and saw that Cruz was still on his leash, standing next to Abe, who was laughing his head off.

Why did he think it was so funny to scare them? Barry wished he could find the courage to step forward and say, "Get off my property!"

He'd practiced that in the bathroom mirror, squinting his eyes to get a fierce look.

But who was Barry kidding? He was about as fierce as one of Mom's peanut butter cookies.

If only Barry was more like his father. Nothing ever got to Roddy Tucker.

And then, as though Barry's thoughts had sent out an SOS, the front door opened and Dad appeared on the porch.

"Hello there, Abraham," he said with a smile.

Abe pulled Cruz closer and lost his usual *what are you looking at?* glare. Suddenly he looked like the old Abe, the pudgy guy in the Saints jersey who tried to show Barry and Jay how to shoot layups.

Dad had that effect on people. He could smile at a T. rex, and next thing, they'd be making plans to have a burger together. Barry's dad was a little famous in the Lower Nine: His band, Roddy Tucker and the Blasters, played in jazz clubs around New Orleans. But Mom said that wasn't why people respected him.

"Your father's got sweet music in his heart," Mom always said. "And everyone can hear it."

Now Dad looked at Barry. "We're leaving in an hour," he said. "You need to pack up. That hurricane's getting nasty. It looks like it might be a direct hit on the city. We're leaving town."

Barry stared at Dad. Leaving town for a hurricane? Not the Tuckers! Never before. Every year a few storms fixed their sights on New Orleans, and they always petered out at the last minute. There hadn't been a bad hurricane in New Orleans in forty years.

Was Dad making this up to get Abe to hustle on home?

"I'm serious," Dad said, reading Barry's doubtful look. "There's a mandatory evacuation. First time in New Orleans history."

"What's that?" Jay asked.

"It means if you can leave, you've got to leave,"

Dad said. "Your mom already called, Mr. Jay. You're heading up to Birmingham."

"What about us?" Barry asked.

"Houston," Dad answered with a sorry smile.

Barry groaned. He loved Mom's Texas cousins, but all of them, five wild little girls and their grumpy mama, lived in a tiny little house. Barry always went home with a whopper headache after visiting them. Dad too. The hurricane must be bad to get Mom and Dad to head to Houston.

Barry looked around his neighborhood — the little houses, the scraggly lawns surrounded by chain-link fences, the palm trees and big oaks. He and Jay used to pretend that those big oak trees were ancient creatures rising from the earth's core.

There were better neighborhoods in New Orleans, and sometimes Mom and Dad talked about moving to a block where police cars weren't always blaring their sirens, where Mom would feel safe walking after it got dark. But the Tucker family had been on this block in the Lower Nine for seventy years. Gramps had helped his daddy build this house back when folks kept hogs in their backyards. Barry couldn't walk half a block without someone shouting hello from a porch and waving him up for a chat and a glass of iced tea.

The Lower Nine was home. And that was that.

Abe started to slink away.

"They're opening up the Superdome, Abraham," Dad called after him. "For folks without cars. You should get your grandma over to the stadium soon as you can."

Abe waved and went on his way.

Dad opened the door to go inside, and the news playing on the radio echoed out to the porch.

"That's right," a man's voice boomed. "This storm is a monster. It's time to leave. Get out now. Get out while you can!"

"You heard the man," Dad said, starting to close the door behind him. "Time to get moving."

CHAPTER 4

Barry's stomach did a few nervous flips. The news reports had been warning about Hurricane Katrina for days, but nobody in Barry's house had been paying much attention. Dad and his band had been playing shows in Atlanta. Mom worked full-time at Cleo's preschool. She also had a little business baking cookies for restaurants in the French Quarter, the fancy neighborhood across the canal. As for Barry, he was totally focused on Akivo. A tornado could have sucked up the house and he wouldn't have noticed.

But now Barry's mind started swirling.

Like everyone in New Orleans, he understood what could happen if a strong hurricane struck. The city was surrounded by water. The Industrial Canal was just two blocks from their house. Big Lake Pontchartrain was up north. The Mississippi River wormed through the middle of the city. And so many canals and channels jutted this way and that, Barry couldn't keep track of them all. Of course there were levees — big walls of dirt and concrete that protected the city from all that water. But some people said that the levees weren't strong enough for a really big storm.

Barry thought of Hurricane Betsy, the storm that hit New Orleans the year before Dad was born. When Gramps was alive, he'd loved telling Betsy stories. He and Gran lived in this same house. The levee broke, and the Lower Nine flooded. Four feet of water filled the living room.

It had taken six months to get everything cleaned up. But Gramps was always proud of how the house held up to the winds.

"Barely lost a roof shingle," he liked to say as he patted the wall like you'd pat the back of a loyal friend.

Those Betsy stories had fascinated Barry when he was little. But they'd always seemed like ghost stories and fairy tales, stories that could never come true.

Now he wondered. . . .

"Barry!" Jay said, waving his hands in front of Barry's face. "Snap out of it!"

"Sorry!" said Barry, shaking himself out of his thoughts.

"What about Akivo?"

They had planned to walk to the post office after school tomorrow and send their package to Acclaim's offices in New York City. Barry had visited New York with Dad the past summer. The president of a famous college there was always inviting Dad to give talks about New Orleans jazz.

"I'll mail him tomorrow," Barry said. "From Houston."

"Let me have him," Jay said, holding out his hand. "I'll mail him from Birmingham."

They stared at each other without budging, until finally Jay blinked.

That settled that. Barry won the stare-out, so he got to mail Akivo.

"Don't let anything happen to him," Jay said.

"I wouldn't!"

They stood there, like they always did before they had to say good-bye. No matter how much time they spent together, it always felt like there was one more idea to talk about, one more joke to tell before they went their own ways.

"Barry, honey, we've got to get ready!" Mom called.

It was time.

Jay raised his hand toward the sky, his pinky

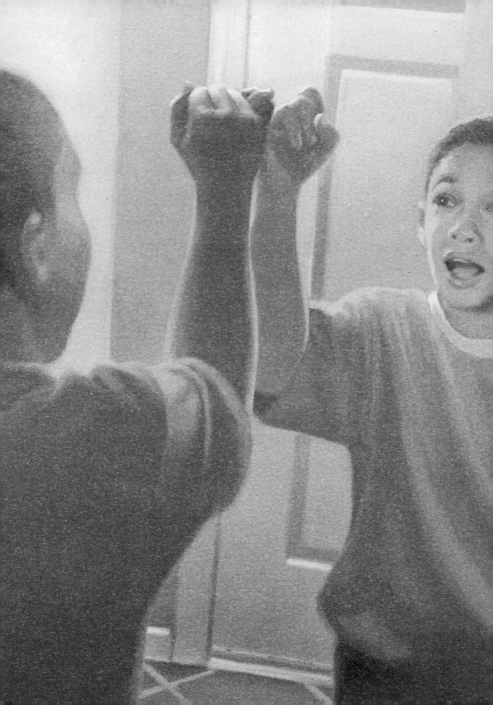

pointing up. It took Barry a few seconds to recognize the special move they'd invented for Akivo so the energy from his secret power star, Beta Draconis, could flow from his pinky into his heart.

Barry raised his hand too, and he and Jay linked their pinkies together in the air.

Barry smiled. For just a few seconds, Barry the believer imagined that he had a power star of his own somewhere.

CHAPTER 5

"Hurricane Katrina is now a Category Five storm, folks," said the man on the radio. "That's the strongest there is. Winds a hundred and seventy-five miles an hour. Waves will be twenty feet high. It's aiming right for our beautiful city. Right for us. This is the storm we've been fearing. It's time to leave. Time to get —"

Mom switched off the radio. "Okay," she said softly. "I heard you. We're leaving."

"Who are you talking to, Mom?" Barry asked.

She looked surprised to see him. "Sorry, baby!" she said, turning and kissing Barry on the cheek. "That man is getting on my nerves." She had three coolers arranged on the floor and was filling them with food for their car trip.

"Are you worried?" Barry asked, brushing some flour from Mom's sleeve. She'd been baking all morning.

"Not at all," she said, but Barry could see she was fibbing. Mom always baked when she got nervous. And she'd packed enough muffins and cookies in those coolers to feed the Saints.

"We're almost ready, right?" she asked.

Barry nodded. He'd helped Dad board up the windows. He'd carried the porch furniture and Cleo's princess house into the shed. "Need anything else?"

"Find your sister," Mom said. "She hasn't been herself all morning. I need you to work some Barry magic on her."

Barry found his sister crying in her bed.

"What is it, Clee?" he asked.

"My princess house!" she wailed. "That lady took it!"

"What lady?"

"Katrina!"

Barry tried not to smile. In that three-year-old brain of Cleo's, Katrina was probably a big fat vampire lady flying through the air.

"Your princess house is safe in the shed," Barry said. "And Katrina isn't a lady. It's just a bunch of clouds. We're not afraid of clouds, are we?"

Cleo looked at Barry with her huge teary eyes. Barry always got a soft feeling in his heart, like the purring of a little cat, when he looked at his sister. Good thing he wasn't a superhero. One look at a crying Cleo and all his powers would be drained away.

"We're having an adventure!" Barry said. "You can't cry on an adventure!"

Cleo gave a big sniff.

"Will Akivo be there?" she asked.

Of course Cleo knew all about Akivo. For weeks, anytime Barry told Cleo a bedtime story, he made Akivo the star. Who rescued Snow White from the evil stepmother? Akivo! Who saved the three little pigs from the big bad wolf? Akivo!

Now Barry put his face closer to his sister's. "I think Akivo will be waiting for us in Houston tonight," he said. He hated tricking Cleo, but it wasn't really a lie. Akivo was always appearing in Barry's dreams. Maybe Cleo would dream about him too.

"To retect us?"

"That's right," Barry said. "He will protect us."

Cleo gave another big, messy sniff and then nodded bravely. "I won't cry," she whispered.

She held out her arms so Barry could pick her up. He pulled her close. She put her head on his shoulder and let him carry her to the car.

Ten minutes later, they were on the road.

CHAPTER 6

They sped through the Lower Nine and crossed the St. Claude Avenue Bridge. They drove past the bakery where Mom had worked before Cleo was born. She'd learned how to make Barry's favorite caramel cake there. Mom's dream was to open her own bakery. They didn't have the money for that now. *But one day,* Mom always said. *One day.* She said those words so often they had become the Tucker family motto.

One day Barry's dad would have a deal with a record label.

One day they'd get rid of their dented old Honda and buy a nice new car.

Maybe even one day Barry wouldn't be so scared of Abe Mackay and his friends.

One day.

They drove a few more blocks, and then Dad pulled up in front of Lightning's, the club where he and his band played most Thursday nights. The owner, Dave Rivet, was one of Dad's closest friends. Barry had known him since before he could walk.

"Why are we stopping?" Barry asked.

"Dad wants to make sure Uncle Dave is leaving," Mom said.

Uncle Dave had spotted their car through the window. He came outside and hustled over to them, his big belly shaking. Uncle Dave had a smile that made you feel like he'd been waiting his whole life to see you.

Dad stuck his arm out the window. Uncle Dave shook Dad's hand and blew a kiss to Mom. He peered into the backseat.

"Hey there, Barry! Hello there, princess!" he boomed, his words stretched out by his thick drawl.

"Grab your bag," Dad said. "We'll make room for you."

Uncle Dave peered at the little space between Barry and Cleo and laughed.

"You gonna tie me to the roof?" he asked.

But Dad's expression was serious. "They're telling everyone to leave," he said. "That means you too."

"Someone needs to keep an eye on our city!" Uncle Dave said. "I'm keeping the club open so folks have a place to go."

"I don't like it," Dad said.

"This place will be fine," Uncle Dave said. "And so will I."

Barry could tell that Uncle Dave wasn't changing his mind.

Dad grabbed Uncle Dave's hand again.

"You take care," Dad said.

"And if you change your mind, I'm right here," Uncle Dave said. "I already told some folks, 'Don't go to the Superdome. Just come to Lightning's.' I have my generator and about a million hot dogs."

"We'll keep that in mind," Dad said.

Uncle Dave put his hands on Dad's shoulders. "And I better see you this Thursday for the show!"

Dad laughed and started up the engine. "Let's hope!"

"Isn't it a bad idea for him to stay?" Barry asked once they'd driven away.

"This neighborhood doesn't usually get flooded," Dad said. "It's a bit higher than the rest of the city."

"And let's face it: If anyone can keep a hurricane away, it's Dave," Mom said.

They sped toward Interstate 10, but the closer

they got, the heavier the traffic became. Soon their car was standing still.

Barry opened his window and stuck his head out. The line of cars and trucks stretched as far as he could see. The hot and sticky air stunk of car exhaust.

Dad clicked on the radio and punched the buttons until he found a traffic report. The news was terrible: Cars were backed up for hundreds of miles on roads leading out of the city.

"This will take all day," Mom said softly, reaching into the cooler and taking out a blue-berry muffin.

Dad patted her leg.

Cleo fussed, and Barry tried to distract her with one of his stories.

An hour went by, and the car didn't budge. Dad had to turn off the air conditioner so the engine wouldn't overheat.

Cleo whined and moaned and finally fell asleep.

Another hour passed. They'd moved just a few feet. Barry's shirt was soaked with sweat.

At this rate it would be hours before they even got onto the highway. And then they had more than three hundred miles to drive.

What if they were stuck in traffic when the storm hit?

Before Barry could ask that scary question, Cleo woke up and started to wail.

And then, as Barry was reaching for her favorite stuffed poodle, a wave of warm soup splashed across his lap. *What in the* . . .

Except it wasn't soup.

Cleo had thrown up. She threw up again, this time into the front seat. And again, onto the floor.

There was a moment of shocked silence, and then Cleo burst into tears.

"Waaaaahhhhhhhhh!" she wailed.

The awful smell rose in the car. Barry put his

hands over his face, which made Cleo scream more.

Mom unhooked her seat belt and scrambled into the backseat. Dad rummaged in the glove compartment and found a wad of napkins. Mom started to wipe off Cleo's face.

"This little girl is burning up!" Mom said.

Barry reached over to feel Cleo's forehead. She was boiling!

"What's wrong?" Barry asked, his heart racing.

"I'm sure she just has a bug," Dad said. "She'll be all right."

Mom gave Cleo a sip of water. "It's okay, baby," she said. "Just try to settle down. You'll feel better soon. . . ."

But Cleo threw up again, and again. She screamed so loudly people in the other lanes peered out their car windows.

Mom and Dad looked at each other, and Barry understood exactly what they were thinking: There was no way they could get on the highway with Cleo that sick.

Sure enough, Dad pulled out of the line of traffic and pointed the car back toward home.

CHAPTER 7

Cleo threw up all day. Barry tried to help keep her calm, but even he couldn't get her to stop crying. Mom managed to talk to their doctor, who had evacuated to Baton Rouge. He said there was a bad flu going around and Cleo wouldn't start to feel better for at least another day.

Mom and Dad talked about going to the Superdome. But the newscaster on TV said there were already ten thousand people at the football stadium, with thousands more lined up around the building.

"We're hearing there is not enough food or water at the Dome," the newscaster said. "And if the power goes off, it's going to be like an oven in there."

Then they showed a man who had been turned away because he wanted to bring his little dog with him.

"They say no pets," the man said, holding the dog up to the camera. "But I can't leave this guy all by himself!"

Looking at those crowds on television, Barry was relieved when Mom and Dad decided they were better off at home.

Throughout the afternoon, Barry kept his eyes on the sky. By six o'clock, the wind had kicked up. The sky turned gray with streaks of silver. But the strangest thing was the silence. Their block was deserted. There were no motorcycles *vroom*ing. No kids laughing and shouting. No music playing or basketballs bouncing. Usually the trees were filled with birds, and frogs chirped from the bushes. But there wasn't a bird in sight, and not a peep was to be heard.

And then, around ten o'clock that night, the wind and rain started for real.

Dad and Barry were settled on the living room couch. The baseball playoffs were on, and Dad had set them up with a feast of chips, salsa, and sodas. Mom and Cleo were fast asleep in Mom and Dad's room.

The wind moaned at first. Then it started to howl, and finally it was shrieking so loudly Dad had to turn up the TV. Barry moved closer to Dad.

Soon there were other noises.

Pom, pom, pom.

"That's just the rain banging against the metal roof on the shed," Dad said.

Ka-bang!

"Whoops, a gutter came loose."

Che-chong!

"There goes part of someone's fence."

Dad sat there calmly, watching the game, munching on chips. Barry remembered their plane ride to New York the past summer. An hour into the flight, they had flown into a thunderstorm. How that airplane bounced up and down! It felt like a giant hand was dribbling the plane like a basketball. Flashes of lightning exploded in the sky. A woman sitting across from Barry burst into tears. The pilot made everyone sit down, even the stewardesses. The plane rattled so badly Barry was sure one of the wings would fall off.

And in all that commotion, Dad had just sat there, reading his book. A few times he'd patted Barry's leg.

"Quite a ride," he'd said, never taking his eyes from the book, never once looking outside at the lightning or craning his neck to see the scared expressions on the stewardesses' faces.

So Barry had kept his eyes glued to Dad's face.

As long as Dad was calm, he decided, he didn't have to worry.

Finally the bouncing stopped. The plane flew out of the clouds and into the clear blue sky.

Later, when they were in a taxi heading into the city, Barry asked Dad how he had stayed so calm. "What were you thinking about?"

"'Blueberry Hill.'"

Barry gave Dad a funny look.

"When I get nervous, I play the song 'Blueberry Hill' in my mind."

Barry knew the song. It was a hit by Fats Domino, the most famous citizen of the Lower Nine. Fats had struck it rich singing songs way before Dad was born. But he never moved out of the neighborhood. Barry and Jay loved to walk by his bright yellow house. Sometimes Fats was out on his porch to wave hello.

Barry watched Dad now as the wind howled and moaned and shrieked.

"Hey, Dad," Barry said, "are you playing 'Blueberry Hill' in your mind?"

Dad laughed.

He put his arm around Barry and pulled him close.

"Nah, I was thinking that wind is making a pretty song."

"Sounds like wolves," Barry said.

"Nah," Dad said.

"Ghosts," Barry said.

"Don't think so," Dad said, listening more closely, tilting his head and half closing his eyes.

Dad clicked off the TV. He reached over and grabbed his trumpet, which he always kept nearby.

The wind shrieked a high note. Dad put his trumpet to his lips and played along.

The wind shifted lower, and so did Dad.

He played softly, along with the wind, until after a while that wind didn't seem so scary, and it actually sounded like a song. Not as pretty as

'Blueberry Hill,' but still a song. Barry almost smiled, imagining Cleo's big fat lady in the sky. Not a vampire, but a pretty singer, belting out her song.

The house shook and rattled, but as Dad's music filled the air, Barry started to feel safe. The lights were bright. Mom and Cleo were cozy in bed. He thought of Gramps patting the walls of the house. In a few hours the sky would turn blue again.

Barry had planned to stay up with Dad, to help him keep an eye out for leaks, to watch over Cleo and Mom. But now he felt tired. All the late nights he'd stayed up working on Akivo . . . and all today he'd been so worried about Clee. . . . Maybe he could take a little rest, catnap like Mom did after dinner, before she started her hours of baking.

Barry closed his eyes . . . drifting, drifting, drifting . . .

And then his eyes popped open.

It took Barry a minute to understand that he had fallen asleep. The room was dark except for the flickering light of a candle on the corner table. The power must have gone out. He squinted at his watch: 6:35. It was morning! He'd slept for hours.

And what had woken him up?

A noise. Not the wind, which was still shrieking and moaning. Not the rain, which hammered down even harder than when Barry had closed his eyes. No. There was a new noise out there. A kind of *whoosh*ing sound.

Barry sat up.

Dad's coffee mug, half empty, sat on the floor. Where was Dad? Was Cleo okay? And what was that strange noise that had woken Barry up?

Barry heard Dad's footsteps upstairs. He stood up, but before he could take two steps, the front door flew open.

A wave of water swept into the house. It

swirled around Barry's legs, knocking him off his feet.

There was a scream, but this time it wasn't the wind.

It was Barry.

CHAPTER 8

"Barry! Barry!"

Dad was pounding down the stairs. He splashed through the water, grabbed Barry by the arm, lifting him up, and pulled him toward the staircase. Furniture and other objects floated around them like bath toys—the new couch Mom had saved for a year to buy, the little square lamp table where Gramps used to play chess, framed pictures of Barry and Cleo from school. The water was rising fast! It was up to Barry's waist by the time they reached the stairs — and it kept getting higher. It was like their house was a bucket being filled up by the biggest hose in the world.

Where was all this water coming from? The water in Gramps's stories hadn't been this wild.

Mom burst out of her room with Cleo in her arms as Dad and Barry made it to the top of the staircase.

She looked down the stairs and gasped. She wrapped her free arm around Barry, pulling him close.

"The levee, Roddy," she said to Dad.

"The levee broke?" Barry asked, picturing the Industrial Canal. The canal was five miles long and very deep. Was all that water pouring into their neighborhood?

Mom and Dad seemed frozen, staring at the rising water.

Panic boiled up inside Barry.

"What will happen?" Barry asked. "What

will we do? What . . ." His voice trailed off. He wasn't even sure he wanted to know the answers to his questions.

They all stood there, huddled together, watching the water move up the stairs.

"We need to go up to the attic," Dad said. "Now."

Dad pulled open the hatch in the ceiling and a blast of hot air came down. Barry had been up there only once in his life. It was a tiny space, dark and hot like an oven, with a ceiling that sloped down so you couldn't stand up straight.

Cleo started to cry.

"No!" she yelled. She tried to run away. "No go up!"

Dad caught her. "Cleo!" he said. She struggled to escape, screaming and squirming. There was no way they could force her up the rickety stairs.

"It's all right," Barry said, taking hold of his sister's hand.

"No! No!" she insisted.

"Clee," he said, working hard to keep his voice steady, "Akivo might be up there."

Cleo sniffed. She let Barry pick her up, and put her arms around his neck. She buried her head in his chest. She still felt feverish. He held her more tightly.

Dad sent Mom up first. Then Barry put Cleo on the ladder and climbed up right behind her. Dad came up last, and they all sat down together in the darkness. There was barely enough room for the four of them, and they were squashed together. The air was so hot it burned Barry's lungs. It stunk like mildew and dust.

He tried not to imagine what was happening just below the attic floor: every single thing they owned—their furniture, Cleo's toys, Mom's cookbooks, Dad's trumpet and all his music— being covered with water.

And Akivo.

He was trapped in Barry's room somewhere.

Lost.

For the past few weeks, thinking about Akivo had given Barry the feeling—a secret, happy feeling—that maybe he wasn't really the scared little kid he saw in the bathroom mirror. He and Jay had created something unique, something special. Somehow, the bright colors of Barry's drawing seemed to have gotten inside him.

But now the bright and powerful feeling drained away. With every minute that ticked by, Barry felt more helpless and terrified. Cleo was whimpering again. Mom held her on her lap, rocking back and forth, singing softly to calm her.

The water was rising past the second floor. They could hear the *whoosh*ing and *bang*ing of furniture below.

What would they do? Where could they go?

Barry's whole body was shaking.

His mind was spinning.

And then Dad leaned in closer.

He put one hand on Barry's shoulder and the other on Mom's.

"I want you to listen carefully," he said softly. "We are all together. And as long as we're all together, we are going to come through this."

Even in the darkness, Barry could see Dad's eyes blazing.

"Soon this will be over," Dad said. "We just have to get through the next few hours."

Mom wiped away Barry's tears.

"We can't stay here in the attic," Dad said. "We're going up onto the roof."

Mom's eyes got wider. She swallowed. "All right," she said.

"But there's no way out," Barry said.

"Yes, there is," Dad said.

"How?" Barry asked.

"Your grandfather."

Barry stared at Dad. Gramps had died three years earlier. Dad wasn't the kind who believed in angels flying around. What was he talking about?

Dad crawled to the darkest corner of the attic. He started back with what looked like a stick.

As he got closer, Barry saw what it was: an ax.

"Gramps always said there'd be another bad storm," Dad said. "He kept this ax up here for forty years. And he made sure I knew about it."

It took Barry a minute to realize what Dad was going to do with that ax.

"Keep your heads down," Dad said.

Mom pulled Barry and Cleo to her.

Dad heaved the ax over his shoulder. With a mighty swing, he smashed the blade into the ceiling.

CHAPTER 9

The water had risen to the attic by the time Dad chopped a hole big enough for them to climb through. The wind screamed and rain poured in.

"Stay together," Dad shouted. "We're going to stay together."

Cleo was so stunned that she stopped fussing. She kept her eyes on Barry's face, and he did his best to look calm, like Dad on the plane.

Dad dragged a trunk under the hole, stepped onto it, and pulled himself onto the roof.

"Barry!" Dad yelled. "Climb up."

Barry stood on the trunk. Dad lifted him by the arms, and Mom grabbed his legs, pushing him up slowly.

Barry gasped when he stuck his head into the storm. The wind was so strong he couldn't keep his eyes open. The rain came down hard and fast, stinging his face like a million bees. Dad held on to Barry, then helped him lie down on his stomach. The wind pushed against Barry's back, gluing him to the roof.

"Stay there!" Dad shouted.

Cleo came up next. Dad laid her down next to Barry. Barry put his arm around her and held on. Soon Barry and Cleo were sandwiched tightly between Mom and Dad.

They lay bundled together like that, not talking. Mom had her arm over Barry's head. Dad's hand rested on his back. Cleo was pushed so close against Barry he could feel her heart beating. He smelled Mom's lemony soap.

Barry kept his eyes closed. But just as he started to feel a tiny bit calmer, there was a loud thud at the end of the roof.

Something had blown through the air and smacked against the house.

Cleo sprang up, struggling to her feet, breaking free from Mom's and Dad's hold.

"Akivo?" she called.

The wind knocked her forward. Mom screamed.

Barry's hand shot out and grabbed Cleo by the back of her shirt. Dad got a grip on her arm. They pulled her back into their huddle.

Barry's heart hammered.

They got Cleo to lie flat again. But before Barry could rejoin their huddle, a gust of wind swirled around him and hit him in the chest. He tumbled onto his side.

"Barry!" Dad called, holding out his hand.

Barry reached out, expecting to feel Dad's grip.

But he slipped back, and his hand sliced through empty air.

He slid down.

Down.

Down.

Down.

The last thing he saw before he fell into the water was the terrified look on Dad's face.

CHAPTER 10

The water seemed to reach up and snatch Barry out of the air. And then he was swept away in a gushing tide. Barry struggled to keep his face above the waves, to keep water from rushing into his nose and mouth. His leg smacked into a piece of wood, but that barely slowed him down. His arm scraped against something sharp. His hand hit something big and furry—a rat?—as the water twisted and turned him and dragged him along.

And then, finally—*crash*—he hit something that stopped him cold.

It was a tree. Almost without thinking, Barry threw his arms around the trunk. The water pulled him, trying to suck him back into the flood. But he held on. He wrapped one leg around the tree, then the other. He hugged that tree so tightly he could barely breathe.

He gathered his strength and then he managed to shinny up the trunk inch by inch. It was an oak tree. All of the branches had been ripped away but one, which rose out of the water. Barry pulled himself up onto it and sat in the V where the branch met the trunk. He hugged the trunk again, bracing himself against the wind.

He couldn't see much in the gray light and the stinging rain. And what he saw hardly seemed real: water in every direction. He felt like he was shipwrecked in the middle of the ocean.

The water was filled with branches and wooden boards and other wreckage from the storm. Barry thought of Atlantis, a city lost under the ocean. He'd read about it in one of his favorite comic books.

Was that what would become of New Orleans?

Barry pressed his cheek against the tree. His entire body ached. His hands were ragged from climbing the tree. He started to cry, his sounds drowned out by the wind.

"Dad!" Barry screamed. "Mom! Cleo!"

He screamed their names until his throat burned.

The wind screamed back at him.

And then he heard a deep groan and a *crack* that echoed above the wind.

A massive shadow loomed over him.

Barry stared in shock: It was a house, pushing through the water like a monster. The windows and doors were gone, and as the house turned slowly in the water, Barry saw that one side had been ripped away.

He had to get out of the way. Now!

Barry jumped into the water, barely missing a big piece of glass. The house hit the tree with a *smash* and a groan and then got stuck there. The current started to drag Barry. He fought against it and somehow managed to swim to the house. He reached up and grabbed hold of a window frame, careful of the jagged glass around the edge.

A piece of wood fell into the water right next to Barry.

Its bright color glowed in the ghostly light: sky blue.

Barry stared at the house.

Could it be?

Yes. It was Abe's house. Abe Mackay's.

And that wasn't all.

The sound of ferocious barking rang out.

Somewhere in that ripped-apart house was Cruz.

The killer dog.

CHAPTER 11

Barry's heart pounded.

That dog was crazy. What if he came after Barry?

Cruz barked some more.

Barry had to get out of here!

But then there was a noise—a whimpering howl. It rose above the wind, and it was the saddest sound Barry had ever heard. Sadder than Cleo's sobbing. Sadder than the song Dad had played at Gramps's funeral. Sadder than Barry's own sobs.

That didn't sound like a killer dog.

It sounded like a dog that was terrified.

Cruz howled again.

Begging. Pleading.

Help me, please, he seemed to be saying. *Help me, please.*

Barry knew what he had to do.

He hoisted himself up, climbed through the window, and eased himself down on the other side. It was very dark, but Barry could see shadowy shapes around him: a couch floating in the corner, a smashed lamp, and a big cabinet lying facedown in the water.

Cruz barked brightly, like he could tell help was on the way.

"Cruz!" Barry shouted.

The dog barked again.

"I'm coming!" Barry called.

Barry waded carefully. His shoes were still floating around in his living room at home; his socks had been ripped off in his ride through the flood. Already his feet were sliced up, and he knew there had to be glass and nails everywhere.

Cruz was whimpering loudly now.

"Don't worry!" Barry called.

Cruz barked like he understood.

Barry made it to the stairway, which rose out of the water. The house was tilted to the side and rocked gently in the waves. Barry had to hold on tightly to the banister.

Cruz was waiting for him in the doorway of Abe's room. His leash was attached to Abe's bed, which Cruz had managed to drag across the room. He was straining so hard to get free that he was practically strangling himself.

Barry paused for a second, thinking of all the scary stories Abe had told him about Cruz. But then he closed his eyes and swallowed hard.

He walked up, reached for Cruz's collar, and unhooked it from the leash.

Cruz leaped up, and for a split second Barry thought he'd made a terrible mistake.

But then Cruz licked Barry's chin. He licked Barry's hands and pushed his head against Barry's leg. Then he sat down and looked up into Barry's eyes. He gave four little barks.

Thank you! he seemed to cheer. *Thank you! Thank you! Thank you!*

Barry bent down next to Cruz and patted him on the head.

"You're welcome," he said.

Cruz gave Barry one last kiss on the nose and then looked at him expectantly.

What now? he seemed to ask. *What should we do?*

And that was when it hit Barry: He wasn't alone anymore. He and Cruz were together.

CHAPTER 12

The back wall of Abe's room was gone. But there was a spot near the top of the stairs where they could escape from the wind and rain. Barry and Cruz sat there for a few minutes, until Cruz started to whimper.

"What's wrong?" Barry asked.

The dog was panting.

"You thirsty? You need water?"

Cruz's tail thumped.

Barry knew that none of the sinks would

work. But maybe there were bottles of water somewhere in the kitchen.

Barry and Cruz made their way down the slanting staircase.

"You stay here," Barry said to Cruz, pointing to the bottom of the stairs. He didn't want Cruz wading through the dirty water.

But Cruz wouldn't stay. He seemed to be glued to Barry's leg.

They waded into the small kitchen. Dishes were floating around their feet, along with boxes and cans of food, but nothing to drink.

Barry yanked open the fridge, and a thrill went through him when he saw two six-packs of Coke, some cheese, hot dogs, bread, and a large bottle of water.

"We're in luck," he said to Cruz.

He looked around for something to carry the food in. He saw a plastic bag floating in the corner and bent down to reach for it. But before he could grab it, Cruz let out a ferocious bark and rammed his body against Barry, almost knocking him down.

A long, dark shape shot out from under the bag and disappeared into the murky water.

A snake!

Barry stood still, frozen in fear.

Was that a water moccasin?

He remembered Gramps's most terrifying Betsy story, about one of his friends who'd been bitten by a water moccasin while making his way through the flooded streets.

"The water was filled with poisonous snakes," Gramps had said. "Lots of people got bit."

Now Barry shuddered.

He grabbed as much food and soda and water as he could carry. He hurried back upstairs, praying that snakes couldn't climb.

There was a metal bowl in Abe's room, and Barry filled it to the top. Cruz emptied it, and Barry filled it up again. Barry drank two cans of Coke. He ripped open the package of hot dogs;

Cruz ate four, one after another. Barry made himself a cheese sandwich and gave Cruz the crusts.

When they were finished, they settled back against the wall. Cruz lay down on top of Barry's legs. He looked up at Barry with a *thank you* kind of look on his face.

Barry stroked his head.

"You're really not a killer dog, are you?" Barry said.

Cruz looked at him and panted a little. Nah. That dog was probably from the shelter in downtown New Orleans. Abe couldn't afford a fancy Chinese army dog even if he'd wanted one. He had made up that killer-dog routine. Another trick to scare the bejesus out of Barry and Jay.

"The storm will be over soon," Barry said to Cruz.

The wind seemed to be dying down a bit.

Cruz was still looking up at him. Barry saw the fear and confusion in his eyes.

What could Barry do?

And then it came to him.

"I found my thrill," Barry sang quietly, "on Blueberry Hill . . ."

Cruz licked Barry's chin. He liked it.

So Barry kept singing—"The moon stood still . . . on Blueberry Hill"—until Cruz put his head on Barry's knee and closed his eyes.

Soon Barry's eyelids started to sag. He stopped singing and leaned back to take a rest, lulled by the gentle rocking of the house and by the song—familiar now—of Katrina's winds and rain.

CHAPTER 13

Cruz was barking. Barking like crazy.

Barry shook himself awake.

Cruz was standing at the edge of the room, where the side of the house had been ripped away. But he was looking back at Barry as he barked.

Come! he seemed to be saying. *Come here and look!*

Something thundered in the sky. The house was shuddering and rocking.

What was happening?

Was it a tornado? An earthquake?

No! It was a helicopter!

It hovered low in the sky, its winds churning the floodwater.

Barry could see the pilot, a young man, through the windshield. He seemed to be looking right at Barry.

"Cruz!" Barry exclaimed. "We're being rescued!"

Barry waved at the pilot. "Here!" he said. "Here! We're here!"

It's over! Barry thought. They'd made it! Soon they'd be out of the flood! He'd be back with Mom and Dad and Cleo!

Barry waved his arms.

The helicopter hovered for a minute longer.

But then it suddenly rose and flew away.

Was it circling? Was it going to come around the other side?

Barry waited. And waited. But the helicopter's

sound grew fainter, and then it faded away completely.

"No!" Barry shouted. "Come back!"

Cruz looked at him, confused.

Barry felt like crying. But he wanted to be strong. For Cruz.

"I'm sorry," Barry said as calmly as he could. "I thought they were coming for us."

The helicopter's winds had stirred up the water, and now the house was rocking so violently that Barry was knocked onto his knees. Cruz yelped. Before Barry could pick himself up, he heard a loud splash.

Cruz had fallen into the water!

Barry dove toward the open side of the house and peered over the edge.

He searched for Cruz, but all he could see was a mess of wood planks and branches. Something poked up in the middle of the debris but then disappeared. It was Cruz! He was tangled up in the mess and struggling to keep his head above the water.

Barry fought the urge to jump right in. It was a ten-foot drop at least. And he had to be careful not to hit anything sharp floating in the water.

"I'm coming, Cruz!" Barry yelled as he eased himself over the side of the house, holding tightly with his hands while letting his legs drop.

He dangled there for a minute, grasping

the edge, staring down into the water, until he spotted a big board floating underneath. Just as it passed, Barry let go. He hit the waves but grabbed hold of the wood before his head went under. He pulled his body onto the board and kicked over to Cruz. The dog was trapped between two branches.

Barry pulled away the biggest branch and grabbed Cruz by the collar.

"I have you," he said, pulling the dog close, hooking his arm around Cruz's body.

Cruz licked him on the cheek and pushed his nose into Barry's ear like he wanted to whisper a secret.

"I know," Barry said. "That was scary. But we're okay. We're okay."

But they weren't okay.

The water was burning Barry's skin. The fumes stung his eyes. Cruz had to be suffering too. They couldn't go back to Abe's broken house. Barry wouldn't be able to lift Cruz through the window. And they couldn't just float like this either.

In the distance, Barry saw the rooftop of a house poking through the water. It was too far to swim to through the poisonous flood. And then he saw a car floating toward them. It was upside down, like a turtle flipped onto its back. Maybe he and Cruz could ride the car to the roof of that house.

Barry kicked as hard as he could, holding Cruz with one hand and the board with the other. They made it to the car and scrambled up onto it. Barry held on to one of the tires, and Cruz stayed close to him. Slowly, the car moved toward the house, almost as though they were driving it. When they were a few feet away, Barry stood up, balancing himself, ready to jump.

"Come on!" he said to Cruz.

And they both leaped off the car and onto the roof.

Cruz slipped, but this time Barry grabbed him

before he fell. They staggered up to a small dry patch near the top of the roof.

Barry sat down, pulling Cruz onto his lap.

He suddenly felt more tired than he'd ever felt in his life. He rested his chin on Cruz's head. Barry could hear dogs barking and howling all around them. He remembered the news report that had said no one could bring pets to the Superdome. There must be hundreds of dogs and cats on their own. Thousands.

And people too. In the distance Barry could hear voices calling for help. He and Cruz weren't the only ones out here.

The light drained from the sky and the sun went down. Barry and Cruz sat slumped together. Neither of them moved. Barry was thirsty but there was no water to drink. Mosquitoes swarmed around them, too many to swat away.

There was nothing to do.

And there was nowhere to go.

CHAPTER 14

The stars came out, more stars than Barry had ever imagined.

Was one of them Beta Draconis, Akivo's secret star?

Beta Draconis was a real star. Barry and Jay had found the name in an astronomy book in the library. They'd learned that there were trillions and trillions of stars in the universe, more stars than grains of sand on every beach and desert on earth. They all seemed to be out that night.

Barry searched the sky and picked out one of the very brightest stars.

"See that, Cruz?" he whispered, pointing into the sky. "That's Akivo's star."

That probably wasn't true. But right then, Barry decided to believe it.

Cruz looked at the sky, and his brown eyes filled up with light. He and Barry leaned their heads together. And soon the sky seemed to wrap itself around them, a glittering blanket to protect them from the awful sights and sounds and smells of their ruined neighborhood.

They sat like that for hours on their little dry patch of roof. A few small boats motored by. Barry called out, but nobody seemed to hear him.

Until, finally, one of the boats slowed down.

It wasn't really a boat. It was more like a raft. A yellow rubber raft with a motor.

The driver was a woman, younger than Mom. She drove the boat right onto the roof and stopped it just a few feet from Barry and Cruz.

"Well, look at you, brave soul," the woman said, her voice low and smooth.

She had very dark skin and huge eyes and dozens of long, skinny braids that seemed to dance around her face. Barry stared at her, sure he was imagining things. She seemed like some kind of fairy—a beautiful fairy in a yellow rubber boat—from one of Cleo's bedtime stories.

But she was real, stepping out of her boat and wading up to Barry in tall rubber boots.

She put a hand on Cruz's head. The dog didn't growl. Like Barry, he seemed hypnotized.

"Who are you?" the woman asked.

Barry's throat was dry and swollen. But he managed to say his name.

"I'm Nell," she said. "Where's your family?"

Barry looked around him at the endless water. His eyes filled with tears.

Nell put her hands on Barry's shoulders.

"How about we get you and your friend out of here?" she asked. "Sound like a plan?"

Barry wiped his eyes and somehow choked out the word "yes."

Barry and Cruz climbed into the boat after Nell.

Nell handed Barry a big bottle of water. She filled a cup for Cruz and held it while he lapped the water up. Barry gulped down his water, almost choking at first. When he was finished, he took a deep breath. He opened his mouth to say thank you, but the only sound that came out was a sob. Suddenly tears were pouring down his face.

He turned away from Nell.

She had called him a brave soul. So why couldn't he act brave?

He was finally off that roof. But now all the terror he'd felt those past hours came back to him, second by second. He felt as if he was

shrinking, as though his fear was boiling up inside him and he was melting away.

"We're going to the St. Claude Avenue Bridge," Nell said. "There will be people to help you there."

Of course there would be. Police and firemen. Doctors and nurses. Barry knew what happened in disasters. He'd seen it on the news. He imagined a big tent on the bridge, with cots set up in neat rows. He would get fresh clothes, more water, good food. The people there would know how to track down Mom and Dad and Cleo.

Barry took a deep breath.

Nell carefully wove the little boat through the maze of uprooted trees and wreckage. People stranded on rooftops called to them as they rode by.

"Help us!"

"We've got a baby here!"

"We're hurt! Please help!"

Nell called back to all of them.

"I'll be back!" she said over and over. "Hang on there! I'll be back."

She whispered a prayer under her breath.

"There are thousands of people stranded, just here in the Lower Nine," Nell said to Barry. "I've already picked up more than thirty people."

Finally the bridge appeared in the distance.

And even from far away, Barry could see that

there were no tents. No flashing lights or police cars or fire engines or ambulances.

Other boats — little boats, like Nell's — pulled up to the bridge, let people off, and then headed back out into the water. There were at least a hundred people packed on the bridge. Families huddled together; old couples sat on the ground; people walked around dazed.

Was Nell really going to leave Barry there by himself?

CHAPTER 15

Nell eased the boat onto the ramp that led to the bridge. Part of the bridge was underwater, but the middle part was high enough that it had stayed dry.

Nell switched off the engine.

"You'll be okay here," she said. "They're bringing people to the Superdome. Someone will help you there."

Barry wanted to believe her. But he knew that even before the storm hit, there had been huge crowds. And not enough food or water. What would it be like now?

And besides, they wouldn't let him in with Cruz.

Barry's fear started to boil up again.

A man came running over.

"Pardon me," he said to Nell, breathing hard. "I'm trying to find my grandmother. She's out there, all alone, up on her roof. I need to get to her, I need . . ."

"I'll take you," Nell said.

The man nodded, wiping away a tear.

"Thank you," he whispered. "Thank you."

Barry knew he had to get out of the boat. Nell had other people to help, like she'd helped him.

Nell leaned over and put her hand under Barry's chin, lifting his face so he had to look at her.

She didn't say anything for a moment. She just looked into his eyes, like she saw something there worth looking at.

"You're strong," she said with no doubt in her voice.

Barry didn't feel strong. His whole body shook as he got out of the boat.

Cruz followed him. They stood on the ramp and watched as the man pushed the boat into deeper water. He climbed in beside Nell.

Nell nodded at Barry, and he suddenly had the idea he'd never see her again. She powered up her engine and the boat pulled away.

As Barry watched Nell disappear, her words echoed through his mind.

You're strong. You're strong.

And soon it wasn't Nell's voice he was hearing in his mind.

It was his own voice.

I am strong. I am strong.

Was he?

He was scared. He was standing there crying, his legs quivering like skinny little twigs in the wind.

But did that mean he wasn't strong?

Barry thought about what had happened to him. How he'd been swept off the roof and carried away. How he'd grabbed hold of that tree and climbed up. How he'd held on tightly against the wind and the rain. How he'd saved Cruz. How they'd made their way through the wreckage to that tiny dry patch of roof.

He'd felt scared the entire time.

But here he was, standing on dry ground. In one piece.

He looked up, and there was his bright star.

Barry's star.

And right then he knew that no matter how scared he felt, he'd find his way.

Or someone would find him.

An hour passed, and Barry heard a familiar voice.

"Barry! Barry!"

And then other voices, calling his name, together, like a song.

Dad reached him first. Then Mom and Cleo.

Their arms wrapped around Barry.

And they stood there together for a long time.

The four Tuckers and Cruz, a tiny island in a huge sea.

CHAPTER 16

SATURDAY, SEPTEMBER 29, 2005
RIVERSIDE PARK, NEW YORK CITY

Barry sat on a bench in the shade. Mom and Dad were standing a few feet away, watching Cleo climb up the jungle gym. Cruz was snoozing at Barry's feet. Barry had a sketchbook open on his lap, and he was looking at his new drawing of Akivo. He'd finished that morning, keeping his promise to Jay. It had been Jay's idea that they could still enter the contest. Jay had even called the Acclaim offices from his grandma's house in Birmingham.

"I told them the whole story," he said. "The man said we can still enter. And they want to meet you!"

Barry wasn't surprised to hear that.

Even four weeks later, Katrina was the biggest story in the country. Every time Barry turned on the TV or got into a taxi with Mom or Dad, another voice was talking about the hurricane.

"This is the worst disaster ever to hit America."

"This is a national tragedy."

"A great American city has been destroyed."

And everyone wanted to hear their story.

The kids at Barry's new school. The man who made their sandwiches at the deli on the corner. Strangers who overheard Mom talking at the bank. They all wanted to know about Katrina. They listened with wide eyes. And then they all

said pretty much the same thing: They said the Tuckers were lucky.

Barry knew that was true.

Mom said it was a miracle that they'd found Barry on the bridge. Some families had been separated for days or weeks. Some still hadn't found each other.

And of course there were people who had died—more than a thousand. They were still finding bodies in attics.

Barry had nightmares about the storm. He didn't sleep much. Even the sound of Dad turning on the shower in the morning made Barry's heart jump.

But yes, he knew he was lucky.

Luckier than the tens of thousands of people who'd been stranded for days in the hot and terrifying Superdome. Or the people who'd been stuck on bridges and highways and rooftops.

The Tuckers hadn't gone to the Superdome.

They had gone to Lightning's. They'd stayed with Dave for two days and then caught a bus to Houston. Dave boarded up the club and went to Baton Rouge. By then even he realized that the city wasn't safe.

The cousins in Houston spoiled them rotten for one week. Mom and Dad talked about moving there, finding an apartment nearby. But then a call came from the president of that famous music college in New York. There was a job for Dad if he wanted, teaching about New Orleans music. There was an apartment too, with furniture and room for the whole family.

A week later, they were here.

Cruz too. He was part of the family now. The Red Cross had helped Dad track down Abe and his grandma in Little Rock, Arkansas. Abe and Barry had talked on the phone. And Abe—the old Abe—had asked Barry if he would keep Cruz.

"He's not a killer," Abe said.

"I figured that out."

They had a good laugh.

And they cried a little too, when they talked about their neighborhood.

Barry hoped he would see Abe again one day.

Mom and Dad came over and sat next to Barry on the bench. Cleo waved from the top of the slide.

Dad looked at Barry's drawing of Akivo.

"That is really something," Dad said.

"Thanks," said Barry, who liked this one even better than the original. Akivo had a sidekick now, a mutt with floppy ears. And he had a guardian angel—a beautiful fairy in a yellow rubber raft.

"He looks like you," Mom said.

"That's right," Dad said. "I see it too."

Barry stared at the picture, and he saw what Mom and Dad meant. Akivo's face—it did look something like Barry's.

"I guess you feel a little like a superhero yourself," Mom said.

"Nah," Barry said, his cheeks heating up.

But really, he did.

Out there in the flood, Barry had discovered some powers of his own.

When it was time to go back to the apartment, Barry went to pluck Cleo off the jungle gym. He heard her singing, "On Blueberry Hill . . . ," and he smiled. Dad told Barry he'd sung that song a million times when they'd been on the roof. Dad had jumped into the floodwater after Barry, but the current had been too strong. He'd fought his way back to Mom and Cleo. The three of them had waited out the storm. Mom said that Dad had called Barry's name so many times that he'd lost his voice.

They walked back to Broadway, Barry pushing Cleo in her stroller.

Mom pointed out a bakery with a HELP WANTED

sign in the window. Dad said they should go to the Bronx Zoo later. Or the American Museum of Natural History.

"There's so much to see," Mom said.

"We have plenty of time," Dad said.

It was true. They had time.

But not forever.

Barry knew they would go back to New Orleans, where they belonged.

When would that be?

When would their city be healed?

Barry didn't ask Mom and Dad those questions.

He already knew the answer.

One day.

One day.

AFTER THE STORM: QUESTIONS ABOUT KATRINA

For many years before Hurricane Katrina, experts had warned that levees in New Orleans were not strong enough to withstand a powerful hurricane. In August 2005, their worst predictions came true. Katrina's 125-mile-per-hour winds sent a gigantic wave of water from the Gulf of Mexico into the canals and lakes surrounding New Orleans. All of that water pushed up against the levees, and many of them failed, some crumbling like the walls of sandcastles. Billions of gallons of water gushed into New Orleans.

Nearly 1,000 people drowned in the first hours of the flooding. Tens of thousands more were like the Tuckers — caught in a nightmare, struggling to survive as water filled their homes. Thousands of people were rescued from their rooftops and attics, often by volunteers like Nell. Nearly 50,000 were stranded in the Superdome in agonizing heat, without enough food or water. It took five full days for help to arrive, and another week before everyone was evacuated from the city.

In the weeks and months after Katrina, many wondered if the great American city of New Orleans would ever recover. There was so much damage. Tens of thousands of houses were destroyed, as well as schools, hospitals, police stations, roads, and businesses. There was no electricity or clean water, and 80 percent of the city was covered with water filled with toxic chemicals and waste. The city's 440,000 residents were scattered all around the country.

But New Orleans did survive. And years later, it continues to recover—building by building, house by house, tree by tree, road by road, family by family. Seventy-five percent of residents have returned. To many visitors, the city seems as vibrant as it always was, with unforgettable music and food, beautiful buildings and gardens, and streets that bustle with energy unlike any other city in America.

But in some of the poorest and hardest-hit neighborhoods, recovery has been painfully slow. If Barry were to come back to the Lower Ninth Ward today, he would see few of his neighbors smiling down from their porches. Much of the Lower Nine is still abandoned. Only 19 percent of that neighborhood's residents have returned.

I've studied dozens of natural disasters over the years—earthquakes and volcanic eruptions and shipwrecks and blizzards and hurricanes. But none of these events made me feel as sad—or as angry—as I felt reading about the horrifying experiences of those who lived through Katrina. Why didn't our leaders do a better job protecting the beautiful city of New Orleans and its citizens? With so many warnings about the dangers of flooding, why wasn't more done to make the levees stronger? Why was help so slow to arrive to the survivors?

As a writer of fiction, I could give Barry and his family a happy ending. But even after reading everything I could find about this storm, I could not find the answers to these questions.

Lauren Tarshis

FACTS ABOUT
HURRICANE KATRINA

- Hurricane Katrina was one of the worst disasters to ever strike the United States. Millions of people in Louisiana, Mississippi, and Alabama lost their homes and businesses. The death toll reached 1,800, including 1,500 who lost their lives in New Orleans.

- More than 340,000 people evacuated from New Orleans before the storm hit. An estimated 100,000 stayed behind. Many of these people were too old or sick to easily make the trip. Others didn't have cars or couldn't afford the costs of evacuation—gas for their cars; train, bus, or plane tickets; hotel rooms. Some thought the storm wouldn't be as bad as predicted.

- Among those who stayed behind was Fats Domino. The famous musician, then

seventy-seven years old, was with his
family in their home in the Lower Ninth
Ward. Like the Tuckers', Domino's house
flooded quickly when the Industrial
Canal levee failed. Mr. Domino and his
family escaped into their attic. They
were rescued the next day, and spent
the rest of the week at the Superdome
before taking a bus to Baton Rouge and
finally landing in Texas. His famous
yellow house still stands, but it is
in ruins.

- Katrina also caused a crisis for the
animals of New Orleans. Pets were banned
from the Superdome, and after the storm,
few people were allowed to bring their
pets on buses leaving the city. Tens of
thousands of pets were stranded without
food and water after the storm.

- In the weeks after the flood, the Humane
Society of the United States organized
the biggest animal rescue in history.
Hundreds of volunteers from all over
the country came to New Orleans. They
broke into boarded-up houses, plucked

dogs and cats from rooftops and trees, and even rescued pigs and goats. Many animals were reunited with their owners. Others were sent to shelters across America to be adopted by new families.

- Americans donated more than $1 billion to help the victims of Hurricane Katrina. Other countries donated too. The largest donor was the government of Kuwait, which gave $500 million.

- Hurricane Katrina was the fiftieth recorded hurricane to pass through Louisiana.

I SURVIVED

THE BOMBING OF PEARL HARBOR, 1941

by Lauren Tarshis

SCHOLASTIC

I SURVIVED

THE BOMBING OF PEARL HARBOR, 1941

by Lauren Tarshis

illustrated by Scott Dawson

Scholastic Inc.

CHAPTER 1

DECEMBER 7, 1941
8:05 A.M.
PEARL CITY, HAWAII

America was under attack!

Hundreds of bomber planes were swarming over Pearl Harbor, Hawaii. They swooped down, machine guns roaring. Bombs and torpedoes rained down.

Explosions ripped through the blue Hawaiian sky.

Kaboom . . . Kaboom . . . KABOOM!

America's mightiest warships were in flames. A curtain of smoke — black and bloody red — surrounded the harbor.

Eleven-year-old Danny Crane had moved to Hawaii just weeks before. Ma had brought Danny to Hawaii to get him out of trouble, away from the crime and the rats and the dirty, dangerous streets of New York City.

But he'd never felt more terrified than he did right now, alone and running for his life. One of the attacking planes had burst out of the smoke and was closing in on him across an empty beach. Danny sprinted through the sand, but there was nowhere to go, nowhere to hide. He peered over his shoulder as the plane flew closer. He could see into the cockpit. The pilot was glaring at him through his goggles.

Rat, tat, tat, tat.

Rat tat tat tat.

Machine-gun fire!

Danny pushed himself to run faster. Searing pain filled his chest as he inhaled the smoky air.

Rat, tat, tat, tat.

Rat tat tat tat.

Sand flew up into Danny's eyes. And then from behind him, a huge explosion seemed to shatter the world.

The force lifted Danny off his feet and threw him onto the ground.

And then Danny couldn't hear anything at all.

CHAPTER 2

ONE DAY EARLIER
DECEMBER 6, 1941
PEARL CITY, HAWAII

Danny stood with his mother at the kitchen window of their tiny house.

Ma put her arm around Danny. "Just look at that view," she said. "Can you believe we live here? I think it's the most beautiful place on earth."

Ma was right; it looked like a postcard out there, with the palm trees swaying in the breeze, the bushes covered with pink and white flowers, and the ocean a sparkling silver strip in the distance.

Danny couldn't stand looking at it.

All he wanted was to be back in New York City, looking out his old apartment window at the jumble of dirty buildings, the smoke thick in the air, the garbage in the streets, and his best friend, Finn, waving to him from down in the alley below.

Ma thought that coming here to Hawaii would give Danny a fresh start. She wanted to get him away from danger and trouble, away from Earl Gasky and his gang.

It was true that Danny and Finn had gotten into trouble sometimes.

But nothing big! Just skipping school and sneaking into movie houses and nabbing an apple or two from the fruit stand.

Sure, they ran with Earl and his gang. Some folks in the neighborhood said Earl was a vicious criminal, that he'd break your legs if you looked at him wrong. But others said he and his guys protected the streets and took care of old ladies. He had always been good to Danny and Finn. He paid them a dollar a day to run errands. He even taught them how to drive one of his cars.

Sometimes it was scary, being on the streets so much, just Danny and Finn. But no matter what they were up to, they always looked out for each other.

Because who else was going to look after them?

Danny's father had been gone since before Danny was born. Ma did her best, but how could she watch over Danny when she was working all the time? She was so tired when she got home from her nursing shifts at the hospital. After kissing Danny hello, she would close her eyes for ten minutes, make their dinner, and then head out to clean offices until midnight.

And Finn's parents had five other kids crammed into a dark two-room apartment. So Danny and Finn stuck together, more than best friends, closer even than brothers. As long as they had each other, they felt like nothing bad could ever happen to them. And nothing ever did.

Until one night two months ago.

Even standing here, looking out on the palm trees, it all came back to Danny. It was like a horror movie playing in his mind. He could hear the screech of the metal on the fire escape breaking away from the building. He heard Finn's shout, and the thud of Finn's body hitting the sidewalk fifteen feet below. He could see Finn lying there on the sidewalk, the blood seeping out of his head, the flashing lights of the ambulance.

And then later, seeing him in that hospital bed, groaning in pain.

It was that night that Ma said they had to leave the city.

"It's time for us to go," Ma said. "Before something terrible happens to you."

When she first told him they were moving to Hawaii, Danny thought she was kidding. Wasn't Hawaii a made-up place, like Shangri-La?

But no.

It turned out it was a bunch of islands owned by America. There was a huge U.S. military base there called Pearl Harbor. They needed nurses at a hospital on an air base called Hickam. They wanted Ma right away.

A week later, the Cranes were on a train heading to San Francisco. From there, they took a ship halfway across the Pacific Ocean, to Oahu, one of the Hawaiian Islands.

Ma kept telling Danny how they needed to put New York behind them.

"We're starting out fresh," she said.

But how could Danny turn his back on Finn?

He couldn't, not when Finn needed him most. Besides, it was Danny's fault Finn got hurt. He was the one who wanted to climb up that fire escape, to explore that abandoned building on 23rd Street. Finn said it was a bad idea, but Danny told him to stop being a sissy. And then, as they were climbing up past the second floor, there was a terrible screech as the rusted metal of the fire escape gave way. Danny managed to climb onto the landing. But not Finn. He fell, crashing onto the cement sidewalk below.

And now Danny was an ocean — and a continent — away. But he had to go back to New York.

A ship called *Carmella* was steaming out of Honolulu Harbor tomorrow morning, heading back to the mainland.

Ma had no idea, but Danny was going to be on that ship.

CHAPTER 3

Ma straightened her white nurse's cap and kissed Danny good-bye. When she opened the door, Danny heard her gasp.

Danny hurried over. Ma said that there was no crime here in Pearl City. Still, Danny was used to being on the lookout for people lurking outside their door, waiting to pounce.

But there was nothing on their porch but a pot of pink flowers, wrapped in a bow.

"Goodness!" Ma said. "That man doesn't quit!"

Every morning for the past week, there had been a present waiting for Ma on their porch. They all came from a man named Lieutenant Andrew Maciel — Mack. He was a B-17 pilot at Hickam Air Force Base, where Ma worked. Danny had met him a few times when he drove Ma home. He came from New York City, so Danny figured he couldn't be all bad.

But then Danny found out he was from that fancy part of New York City called Sutton Place. Danny and Finn hated those rich Sutton Place kids, with their chauffeured cars and snooty expressions.

Danny hoped Ma wasn't sweet on this guy.

She smelled the flowers and smiled a little before handing the pot to Danny.

Then she kissed Danny again and headed on her way. Danny could hear her humming until she disappeared around the corner.

He brought the flowers to their little patio around back. He sat down on one of their rickety little chairs. The sun felt good on his face, and there was a warm breeze off the ocean. Maybe he'd miss the smell of the air here when he got back to New York — it smelled sweet, like sugar cane and pineapple. One thing he'd definitely miss was the sound of the bells that rang out every hour from the battleships anchored in Pearl Harbor.

The naval base was just five minutes from their house. There had to be a hundred warships crowded into the harbor with their guns ready to blast away. The best were the eight battle-ships. They were huge — like skyscrapers turned on their sides. Ma said the battleship guns were so powerful that one blast could blow an entire house to smithereens.

Danny wished he could tell his teacher in New York about those ships.

Most teachers at their school hadn't bothered

much with Danny and Finn. But Mrs. Mills was different. When it was too hot or cold outside, Danny and Finn would offer to wash Mrs. Mills's chalkboard for her. She always said yes, and she always happened to have a Thermos of lemonade or hot chocolate with just enough for them. She also had a big world map on the wall of her classroom. They could point to any country and Mrs. Mills could tell them everything about it.

More recently, Mrs. Mills had talked to them about the wars happening all around the world. She pointed to Asia, where Japan was fighting China. She pointed to Europe, where there was a maniac named Adolf Hitler in charge of Germany. He was sending his armies out to conquer every country he could.

Mrs. Mills hated Hitler.

"The world has to stop that monster," she told them. "He's marching across Europe now. But you watch. If we don't stop him, he'll want

America next. He'll want to hang a German flag over the Empire State Building."

Danny and Finn didn't like that idea one bit. And then one day they heard a shocking rumor: One of Earl's guys said that German U-boat submarines were sneaking around the waters just off Coney Island, in Brooklyn.

That did it! Danny and Finn skipped school

and hopped a subway down to Brooklyn. They sat there all day, freezing on Coney Island Beach, watching out for U-boats. They had no idea what a U-boat would look like. But that didn't matter. Finn brought his baseball bat. If a German soldier had tried to step onto the sand, Finn was ready to clobber him.

They didn't spot a U-boat. But the day wasn't a total waste. When Mrs. Mills heard that they'd skipped school to protect America, she gave them both an automatic 100 percent on their spelling tests. Finn grinned so big you could see the gold tooth from when he broke up a fight between two of his little brothers.

Thinking about his good times with Finn gave Danny a strange feeling. Of course Danny never cried — he was no sissy. And he'd learned a trick when he was younger. On those nights when he was alone in the apartment, wishing Ma wasn't gone so much, wondering why his father had left them, he'd push all the feelings down, and then pack them tight together. He could almost imagine them somewhere deep inside him, a hard ball of ice. Lately that cold hard place had grown so big Danny almost felt numb. But it was better than lying around crying.

Now Danny stood up, cursing himself for wasting time. He had to pack, write his note to Ma, get himself ready for the long journey back to New York City, to Finn.

But then he heard a commotion in his back-yard.

There was a crash, a strange squeal, and an earsplitting scream.

CHAPTER 4

Danny flung open the back door.

Ma's new pot of flowers lay shattered on the ground.

Was someone in trouble?

Or were robbers planning to break in?

Danny picked up a broom, ready to strike.

The yard was small, just a patch of grass surrounded by a tangle of bushes and palm trees. He didn't see anyone, but then he caught sight of a small dark head poking out from behind one of the thick bushes.

Danny put down the broom and walked over. It was a little kid, maybe three years old.

What the heck was he doing here all by himself?

"Ahhhhhhhhhh!" the kid screamed.

Was the kid hurt?

"Hey!" Danny said.

The kid turned around.

He was grinning like a monkey standing on a mountain of bananas. And he was clutching a little animal of some kind.

"Puppy!" the kid said.

Danny studied the animal. It was very small and black except for one white ear.

He didn't want to break the kid's heart, but he was pretty sure it wasn't a puppy. It looked more like a rat.

"My puppy!" the kid said, hugging the poor

ugly critter so tight Danny was sure it would pop like a balloon.

Danny looked around. The kid was too young to be wandering around on his own.

"Who are you?" Danny said, bending down to look the kid in the eye.

"Aki!" he said. "Who you?"

"I'm Danny," said Danny.

"Danny see my puppy?"

Aki held out his poor squished pet like he wanted Danny to give it a big smooch.

And then the kid's eyes got huge. He pointed to something over Danny's shoulder.

"Monster!" he said.

Danny spun around and there, moving toward them, was the ugliest animal Danny had ever seen in his life. It was black, the size of a huge dog, with wiry bristles, a pig's snout, and two huge spiked tusks sprouting right from its face like swords.

It *did* look like a monster.

The animal grunted and snorted as it stared at Aki with beady black eyes.

Prepare to die! it seemed to be saying.

"Put down the puppy!" Danny said, suddenly understanding: That was a mother monster, and she thought Aki was stealing her baby.

"My puppy!" Aki screamed.

Danny pried the baby out of Aki's sticky hands. He gently placed it on the ground. The mother rushed up to it, nudged it with her nose, and gave a loud squeal.

"Okay," he said, bending down and speaking softly to Aki. "Let's go."

Aki screamed again, right into Danny's ear.

"My puppy!" Aki howled, lunging over to reclaim his pet.

The mother monster gave out a high-pitched roar.

Aki screamed right back.

This kid really was crazy!

Danny tried to grab Aki, but he pulled away.

The animal charged, its sharp tusks aimed right for Aki's stomach.

CHAPTER 5

Danny managed to grab Aki by the seat of his pants and hoist him up just in time.

One of the monster's tusks tore through Danny's pant leg. Amazingly, it missed his flesh.

Danny jerked back his leg, ripping his pants away from the tusk. He almost fell, but he regained his balance and kept his hold on Aki, who was still screaming for his puppy.

With Aki held high, Danny ran across the yard and into the house, slamming the door.

"My puppy!" Aki screamed. "My puppy!"

"No," Danny said, putting the kid down and blocking the door. "That's not yours. That's the monster's baby."

"Not Aki's puppy?" Aki said, his eyes getting bigger. There were tears now.

"Sorry, little guy," Danny said. "But that puppy has to be with its ma."

"Aki want puppy," he said, throwing his arms around Danny and burying his face in Danny's legs.

This kid was a stitch. Danny had always wanted a little brother, someone to trail along with him and Finn, someone to keep him company when Ma was working.

"Where's your ma?" Danny said.

"Mama mad at Aki," Aki said.

And sure enough, just then Danny heard someone shouting Aki's name.

Danny stuck his head out the window.

"I got him!" he called.

A moment later, he and Aki were standing on the porch with Aki's mother.

Danny guessed she and Aki were Japanese. There were people from all over the world living here — just like in New York City. Lots of the people in Pearl City were originally from Japan, Ma had said.

"Aki!" his mother scolded. "You cannot be running away like this!"

"I sorry, Mama," he said in a voice sweeter than a chocolate doughnut. He wrapped his arms around his mother's legs and gazed up at her with an angelic smile.

Danny saw how the anger in Aki's mother's eyes melted away.

This little kid was *good*.

She looked at Danny and smiled. Even though she looked nothing like Mrs. Mills, there was something about her that reminded Danny of his teacher — a look in her eyes, like she could read his mind and liked what she saw.

"Thank you," she said. "My son is a wanderer. The minute I turn my back, he sneaks away."

"We saw monster!" Aki said.

"A monster?" the woman said, raising her eyebrows.

"It looked like a hairy pig," Danny said. "With horns."

"A wild boar?"

"Monster hurt Danny," Aki said, pointing to Danny's torn pants.

"Goodness!" Aki's mother said with surprise. "Did he really hurt you?"

"Just my pants," Danny said. He decided not to tell Aki's mother how the boar almost turned Aki into a shish kebab.

"But it's very unusual for a boar to attack," said Aki's mother.

"Aki got hold of one of its babies," Danny said.

"Puppy." Aki smiled. "My puppy!"

Aki's mother shook her head.

"Aki sees the beauty in everything," his mother said. "Even a wild boar. But one of these days, Aki, you're going to end up in big trouble."

"He's a good kid," Danny said, wanting to protect his new friend.

"I good boy!" Aki said, puffing out his chest.

Danny and Aki's mother looked at each other, and they both laughed.

The sound startled Danny. He hadn't laughed since the night Finn fell.

Aki stared at both of them, trying to see what was funny.

Then he grabbed Danny's hand and started pulling with all his might.

"Danny come!" Aki said. "Danny come over!"

Danny opened his mouth to say "no thank you." But Aki kept shouting, "Danny come!" and pulling on his hand, trying to haul him up the hill. For such a shrimp, the kid was a real muscleman.

"You might as well come," Aki's mother said. "I have lunch just about ready. And as you can see, my son doesn't take no for an answer."

CHAPTER 6

Before Danny really understood what was happening, Aki had dragged him up to their house, if you could call it a house. It was smaller than the Cranes' house and made of cement, with a metal roof. Still, there was something nice about it—the white flowers climbing up one of the walls, the neat vegetable garden planted in front. Aki's mother had introduced herself on the way up—she was Mrs. Sudo. She explained that Aki's father was a fisherman out on a three-day trip. He'd be back tomorrow afternoon.

Mrs. Sudo had Danny sit down at a little wooden table in front of the house. Aki scrambled onto his lap. He stayed there as Mrs. Sudo served lunch. The food was weird — bowls of rice with fish in a salty sauce — but not so bad, especially the bright orange fruit for dessert. It tasted sweet as a lollipop.

After they ate, Aki curled up on Danny's lap. Danny thought he would fall asleep, tuckered out by all of the excitement.

But then a formation of bomber planes flew over them. There were always military planes crisscrossing the skies above Pearl Harbor. There were army and navy airfields all around the harbor, not only Hickam, where Ma worked.

Aki leaped up.

"B-18!" he shrieked. A minute later, three more planes appeared.

"A-20!" he shouted.

And finally, "Danny! B-17! Flying Fortress! B-17 Aki's favorite plane!"

"Aki knows all the planes," Mrs. Sudo said, putting another plate of orange fruit in front of Danny. "Aki, why don't you show Danny your book?"

Aki hopped off Danny's lap and shot into the house. He reappeared a minute later and handed Danny a worn sketchbook. He grinned proudly as Danny opened it. Danny stared at the pages, each one filled with perfect drawings of bomber planes and warships.

"You drew these?" Danny said in amazement.

"My papa!" Aki said.

"My husband drew those," Mrs. Sudo explained. "When he's home, he takes Aki down to the docks. They'll sit there for hours."

"He's really good," Danny said.

"He's an artist." Danny could hear the pride in Mrs. Sudo's voice. "Fishing is just his job."

B-17 BOMBER,
"FLYING FORTRESS"

P-26
(MOSTLY
TRAINE

BELLY BALL
TURRET →

A-20
"HAVOC"

P-40

B-18 BOMBER

"I wish I could draw," Danny said.

Actually he already could draw, a little bit. Mrs. Mills got him a sketchbook and told him to practice, but he never made much progress.

"My husband would love to help you learn," Mrs. Sudo said. "Is your father in the military?"

"No," Danny said. "It's just me and my ma. She works as a nurse at Hickam. We moved here from New York City a couple of weeks ago."

"Your mother's very brave, to come all this way to start a new life."

Danny had never really thought of it that way. Ma had looked so scared after Finn fell. But he guessed it was brave, to leave the city she'd lived in her whole life, to travel halfway around the world.

"She's lucky to have a boy like you," Mrs. Sudo said.

The words hung in the air a minute—*a boy like you*—and then they seemed to slap Danny in the face.

Tears came into Danny's eyes, but he had no idea why.

Somehow, being here with Aki and Mrs. Sudo, some of that ice inside him had melted.

He had to get out of here.

He stood up so quickly that he dropped Aki's book onto the floor.

"Thank you for lunch," he said, picking up the sketch pad and handing it to Aki. "But, uh, I have to go."

"Danny!" Aki shouted. "Stay!"

"You're welcome to stay the afternoon," Mrs. Sudo said. "Until your mother returns from work."

"I'm sorry," Danny said. "I'm sorry, but . . . I have to leave."

And without even a wave good-bye, he ran down the hill and into his house.

CHAPTER 7

Danny lay in his bed, listening to the morning birds sing outside his window.

The *Carmella* was leaving in two hours. He was all ready for the trip. He had packed a small bag. He had written the note to leave for

Ma. And he had the entire plan laid out in his head.

Stowing away on the *Carmella* would be easy—one of Earl's guys did it once when he was younger: stowed away to Cuba to track down an old girlfriend. You had to be smart about it—dress nice, wash up, pretend you were visiting some passengers. Then, when the bell rang for all the visitors to leave, you had to find a good hiding place, like a storage closet, or a lifeboat, if you could sneak in without someone seeing you. Anywhere you could stay out of sight for at least a day, until the ship was far out to sea.

After that, if you got caught, there wasn't much the crew could do. They wouldn't toss Danny overboard. He'd already figured out his sob story: He was an orphan, trying to get back to New York to be with his cousin Finn. He might even mention the name Earl Gasky.

People had heard of Earl, even outside of New York. Danny heard that he was even friends with some guys in the FBI. Earl could get people to do all kinds of things, even give a kid a ride across the Pacific.

The trip would get trickier when the boat docked in San Francisco. Danny would have to slip away before the police got there. He'd have to get himself to the freight train yards. Riding freight cars wasn't so easy. Danny had heard bad stories about the "yard bulls," the guards who searched the sidings for train jumpers. They'd beat you up and then toss you through the doorway of the police station.

But none of this scared Danny.

So what was he doing still in bed?

He should have gone to the Honolulu port right after Ma left for work at 7:00.

But he couldn't bring himself to leave. All night, he'd been hearing Mrs. Sudo's voice in his head.

Your mother is lucky to have a boy like you.

A boy like Danny.

What kind of boy was he?

A boy who didn't turn his back on his best friend.

But did that mean he was a boy who would leave his ma?

All these weeks he'd been thinking about doing what was right for Finn, but now he couldn't stop thinking about Ma. What would she do when she discovered that Danny was gone? He couldn't even imagine it, how frantic she'd be.

All night he'd been tossing in his bed, feeling torn in two.

He was lying there, his thoughts seesawing back and forth, when a familiar voice rang out.

"Danny! Danny, come!"

Aki was outside again.

Now his plans would really be messed up!

Danny climbed out of bed. He quickly dressed

and went to the door. Aki was standing there by himself.

"Aki," he said. "What are you doing here?"

The kid wasn't wearing his crazy monkey grin. His face looked dead serious.

He pointed up to the sky and said in a soft and scared voice, "Airplanes."

CHAPTER 8

"Come on," Danny said, picking Aki up. "We need to get you back home. Your mama will be very worried."

"Airplanes," Aki said, looking into the sky.

"Aki, you have to go home, come on, you have to . . ."

Aki put his hand on Danny's mouth, silencing him.

"Shhh!" he said. "Airplanes."

Danny almost pulled Aki's sticky hand off his face.

But then he heard a sound he'd never heard before.

A buzzing sound, like there was a giant swarm of bees closing in.

Danny followed Aki's pointed finger. And then he saw it in the distance — what looked to be an enormous flock of gray birds flying toward Pearl Harbor.

As the gray spots grew larger, Danny could see that Aki was right. They were airplanes. More than Danny had ever seen. And then he saw even more, coming in from another direction.

There must be a drill going on. The navy and army were always practicing. There had been a drill at Hickam last week, when fifty sailors had to pretend to be wounded. Ma came home exhausted and covered in fake blood.

Whatever game these planes were playing, Danny didn't have time to watch them, not if

he planned to catch the *Carmella*. He'd already wasted too much time bellyaching in bed.

"Come on," Danny said, holding out his hand. If he hurried, he'd get Aki home and then be able to hitchhike to Honolulu. He could still make it to the port in time.

Then, when they were almost up the hill, an enormous *BOOM* shook the ground.

And then another.

Danny stopped short.

"Fire!" Aki shouted.

Flames were rising from one of the battleships.

What kind of drill was this? Had a pilot crashed or dropped a bomb by mistake?

Danny stopped moving. Aki wrapped his arms around Danny's neck. Danny could feel the little boy's heart beating, like tiny running footsteps.

Together they stared at the scene over the harbor.

The planes were flying so low they seemed to skim the tops of the taller ships.

Kaboom!

Another explosion rang out.

Sirens began to howl.

Boom . . . boom . . . BOOM . . . BOOM!

The sky was filling with black smoke.

"My ships," Aki whispered.

A feeling of dread came up through Danny, a black and swirling feeling, like on that night with Finn, when he'd first heard the metal of the fire escape start to give way. He knew something horrible was happening, something beyond his worst nightmares.

He gripped Aki tighter.

"Aki," Danny said. "Are those B-17s?"

Aki shook his head.

"Are they B-18s?"

Again Aki shook his head.

"A-20s?"

"Not Aki's planes."

And that's when Danny knew.

It was Hitler! Germany was attacking! Just like Mrs. Mills had said it would!

More explosions rang out. The air filled up with a horrible smell.

A voice rang out.

"Aki!"

Mrs. Sudo came running down the hill.

"Thank goodness!" she cried, grabbing Aki and hugging him.

"The Germans are attacking us," Danny said.

Mrs. Sudo turned to Danny.

She had tears in her eyes.

"No, Danny," she said. "Those are not Germany's planes."

"Who else could it be?" Danny said. Who else was crazy enough to bomb Pearl Harbor?

"Those are Japanese planes," Mrs. Sudo said.

Japan?

What had America done to Japan?

Why would they want to destroy all of those ships?

There were no answers, just more explosions, more of that black, bloody-looking smoke.

Aki was crying.

"Come," Mrs. Sudo said, grabbing Danny's hand. "I know somewhere we can go, in case . . ."

Danny knew what she wasn't saying: *In case the planes started bombing their houses too.*

They hurried up and around the back of the Sudos' little house. Danny helped Mrs. Sudo open the wooden door that led to her root cellar — not much more than a hole in the dirt. Mrs. Sudo went down the narrow wooden stairs first, and Danny handed Aki to her.

"Come, Danny," Mrs. Sudo said.

But Danny was staring out over the smoke and flames.

Somewhere in the middle of all that was Hickam.

And somewhere at Hickam was Ma.

"I need to find my mother," he said.

"No! Your mother would want you here! Please stay! She would want you to be safe!"

Danny knew that was true.

But he ran away anyway, down the hill, toward the fires, toward Ma.

CHAPTER 9

As Danny hurried past his house, he barely recognized his new neighborhood.

Cars sped by. People were running through the streets, shouting. A truck rumbled past with a man hanging out the passenger window. He was yelling through a bullhorn.

"All military personnel! Report to your posts! We are under attack! We are under attack! This is not a drill! America is under attack by Japan!"

Military men were rushing out of their front

doors, buttoning their uniform shirts as they ran, calling out good-byes to their wives and children.

"Take the kids up to the cane fields!" one yelled. "Hide if you have to! I'll find you when this is over!"

Some of the ladies stood in the doorways and cried.

Danny ran across the street to the beach. Through a curtain of smoke across the harbor, Danny could see the planes pummeling the battleships, flying low, firing their guns, and then circling back for another attack.

The noises pounded in Danny's ears.

Boom. Boom. Boom. BOOM!

Rat, tat, tat, tat.

Keeeee POW!

Where was Ma?

Was she safe in the hospital, or were the Japanese trying to blow that up too?

How would he get to her?

Tears came into Danny's eyes.

And then suddenly something appeared through the smoke. One of the planes had peeled away and was heading his way.

Danny expected it to loop around and head back to the harbor.

But it was coming toward the beach.

Straight for Danny.

Danny stood there, frozen by fear. He watched as the plane got closer and closer, until he could see the pilot. The man looked very young. He had a white rag tied around his head. He wore goggles. His plane had big red circles on both sides.

Danny remembered Mrs. Mills's classroom. She had pictures of all the flags of the world lined up. Japan's was a white flag with a red ball in the middle.

The red ball was supposed to be the rising sun, Mrs. Mills said.

But now all Danny could think of was a ball of fire.

There was a terrible roaring sound.

Rat, tat, tat, tat.

Rat tat tat tat.

Sand flew up all around Danny. Machine-gun fire! Why was the pilot shooting at Danny?

Danny ran across the sand. But there was nowhere to hide.

The roar of the plane got louder as Danny ran.

Rat, tat, tat, tat.

Rat tat tat tat.

Behind him, there was an explosion so enormous that the ground beneath Danny seemed to rise up.

His head smashed against the sand.

And then he couldn't see anything at all.

CHAPTER 10

8:45 A.M.

Danny wasn't dead.

His head felt like it had been split in two.

His hands and knees throbbed.

His mind swirled.

His mouth was filled with sand and blood; he'd bitten his tongue. His ears were ringing.

But he was all in one piece.

He had no idea how much time had passed since that plane appeared.

The plane was gone now. The attack seemed to be over.

As his mind cleared, he managed to sit up. Over the harbor, one of the battleships was a ball of fire. That was the huge explosion: An entire battleship had been blown apart.

That's what had knocked him down.

Danny finally struggled to his feet and staggered across the beach toward the road.

He saw a car parked at the edge of the beach, the front end partially hidden in a prickly bush. It was covered with bullet holes. The back window was shattered. He didn't see anyone; probably the driver had run away. Danny wondered if the guy would mind if he borrowed it. Earl had not only taught Danny and Finn how to drive. He'd shared a secret for starting a car engine without a key.

But as Danny got closer to the car, a man's

face appeared through the shattered driver's window.

"Hey, kid," he called. "You okay?"

Danny couldn't believe his eyes. It was his mother's friend, Mack.

"Dan!" Mack said. "Is that really you? Are you okay? Were you hit?"

"I'm okay," Danny said.

"Where is your mother?" Mack asked.

"She's at the hospital," Danny said, his voice shaky. "At the base. I think it was hit. I need to get there."

Mack looked nothing like a fancy Sutton Place man trying to impress Danny's mother. His expression was fierce and determined.

"Let's go," he said. "That's where I'm heading. You come with me. We'll find her."

When Danny got into the car, he noticed blood spattered on the doors. Mack's arm was bleeding badly.

"You're hurt," Danny said.

Mack glanced at his arm. "I got grazed by a bullet," he said. "I've had worse."

He pulled the car up onto the road and they drove off.

"They caught us by surprise," Mack said. "The Japanese blindsided us."

"Why?" Danny said.

"To knock out our ships and bombers," Mack said. "To cripple our entire Pacific fleet. That way they can take over whatever they want in the Pacific—China, the Philippines, Korea. Japan is a small country, but they want to be powerful. They need more land. So they're taking over other countries, like Hitler has been doing in Europe. And now we won't be able to stop them."

"But didn't we know they would do this?" Danny said. "Shouldn't we have known?"

"Some people talked about it," Mack said. "But nobody thought they could pull it off."

Mack looked at Danny.

"I'll tell you what," he said. "The Japanese made a mistake. A big mistake. They have no idea what they've started. This country is going to rise up and crush them. You'll see."

"And what about Hitler?" Danny said.

"Him too," Mack said.

Mack sounded so sure. And Danny wanted to believe him. But now he was thinking about Mrs. Mills's map, stretched across the classroom wall. How could America fight two wars on opposite sides of the world?

As Hickam came into view, Danny could see smoke and flames rising from the base.

Mack swore under his breath.

They pulled up to the gate, which was blocked by a smashed car, still smoldering.

"Let's go," Mack said, opening his door.

Danny followed Mack around the burning car and toward the gates at the base.

Ahead, the base reminded Danny of a photo he'd seen in *Life* magazine of a town that had been hit by a tornado. There was wreckage everywhere — twisted metal all over the ground, shattered glass, pieces of burned wood. He stepped over a tattered hat. He wondered what had happened to the man who'd been wearing it.

Some of the buildings had been destroyed; two were still burning. The air was hard to breathe. It smelled like burned rubber and plastic. And everywhere he looked, Danny saw wrecked planes. Some were cut right in half.

Two armed guards stood at the gate. They both saluted when they saw Mack, and then they both started talking at once.

"We were hit bad, sir!"

"We've lost about a dozen men, sir!"

"About a hundred are wounded."

"They destroyed the barracks and the mess hall. Two hangars are gone."

"We lost a lot of planes, sir. They torched them right on the runways."

Mack listened closely to the rush of information. Finally he held up his hand to quiet the men.

"Did we get any planes into the sky?" Mack asked.

"No, sir."

"Hospital okay?" Mack said, reading Danny's mind.

"Hospital's fine, sir. No hits. They're treating the wounded."

Danny closed his eyes with relief. And then he heard a ferocious roar.

Another wave of Japanese bomber planes roared out of the sky, whistling through the smoke, right over their heads.

Bombs started pouring down.

CHAPTER 11

In an instant, a bomb exploded on the runway. A man disappeared in a blaze of flames and black smoke.

Danny and Mack and both guards hit the ground hard.

Mack came over and shielded Danny's head and shoulders with his body. He waited for a lull in the explosions and then he scrambled to his feet. He grabbed Danny's hand, yanking him up.

"We need to get out of here!" he shouted to the guards. "We need to find cover!"

Turning to Danny, Mack yelled, "Come on!" Mack held Danny's hand tight as they ran. "Keep your head down!"

But where could they go?

Bombs were exploding all around them.

Boom! A truck exploded.

Boom! Three men fell to the ground.

A plane flew in low.

Pom, pom, pom, pom, pom.

A spray of bullets ripped apart a car.

Soldiers were crouched behind bushes and under cars. Some had small handguns and were firing uselessly into the sky. One soldier threw rocks. Danny couldn't believe it; did they really think that would stop the planes?

But he understood too. There was nothing they could do.

Mack dragged Danny behind what was left of a huge airplane hangar. Through the enormous holes in the walls, Danny saw U.S. bomber planes — shattered and burning. In the lawn behind the hangars, bombs had blown craters into the grass. Mack pushed Danny into one and then jumped in after him.

"Get down!" Mack said.

Danny curled up against the dirt wall, and Mack crouched next to him, shielding Danny with his body.

Men shouted all around them.

"He's hit!"

"Watch out!"

"We need help!"

"They're coming in low!"

Danny pressed his head against the side of the hole. Mack held him tight.

"It will be over soon!" Mack said.

But the planes kept coming. Danny peered up, knowing he'd never forget the sight of those planes. They were small and gray, like killer birds.

A whistling sound cut though the air, and then—

Kaboom!

Dirt, rocks, and metal rained down on them. Something sharp stabbed Danny in the calf. He reached around and pulled out a small piece of metal, tossing it behind him.

Danny closed his eyes tight, praying for the attack to stop.

Suddenly he thought of Finn. He could almost feel that Finn was with him there, telling him to be brave. The feeling was so powerful—it filled Danny's entire body.

And finally the thundering stopped.

The attack was over. The roar of the planes was replaced by the shouts of men.

Danny turned, and Mack fell back, his eyes dazed.

"I'm hit," he rasped. "My back. I think it's bad."

Danny looked at Mack's back. His stomach

heaved as he saw a jagged wound. And more blood than he had ever seen.

Mack wouldn't last long, bleeding like this.

A blond soldier appeared above the crater. His glasses were cracked and he had a gash on his face.

"Everyone all right here?" he asked.

"He's bleeding bad, sir!" Danny said.

The soldier shouted for help, and within seconds he and another man were helping Danny lift Mack from the crater. Mack winced in pain as they pulled him onto the grass and laid him on his side. The soldier pressed against the wound with his bare hand, trying to slow the bleeding.

"Hang on, sir," the blond soldier said. "Help is on the way."

But Danny didn't see any help.

"Are there ambulances?" Mack asked.

"All the ambulances are out, sir."

Mack nodded grimly. His jaw was clenched and his face was very pale.

"What about that car?" Danny asked, pointing to a red Studebaker parked next to the hangar.

"That belongs to our colonel," the soldier said.

Danny leaped up and rushed to the car.

"Wait!" the soldier shouted.

But Danny ignored him.

The car had been spared any hits. It barely even had a scratch.

Danny lifted the hood and studied the engine. He easily found the two ignition wires Earl had shown him.

"You never know when you need to get some-where quick," Earl had said with a smile.

As usual, Earl had been right.

Danny carefully touched the wires together. The engine sputtered to life.

Danny flung open the door and jumped inside. He drove the car around holes and chunks of glass and metal, pulling up as close as possible to where Mack lay.

The blond soldier looked worried. But Mack managed a smile.

"Good work, kid," he said. "I won't ask where you learned how to do that. But I'm darned glad you did."

Danny and the soldier helped Mack into the car.

"Go!" the blond soldier said. "The hospital is half a mile down, on the right."

"Wait," Mack said. "There are other guys who need help. We're not leaving until the car is full."

Five minutes later, there were two more wounded men in the car. One man had so much blood on his face that Danny couldn't tell what he looked like. The other was holding on to his leg like it might fall off.

Danny drove as fast as he could to the hospital. The road was cratered and filled with burned wreckage. Once he had to get out and drag a huge piece of a plane out of the road. But finally he made it.

When they got to the hospital entrance, Danny blared the horn, signaling for help.

While they waited for help, Danny turned and looked at Mack.

Mack's eyes were fluttering. Danny wasn't sure what to do. And then he reached over and grabbed Mack's hand.

"Mack," he said.

"What?" Mack rasped.

He could only think of one thing to say.

"I'll make my ma have dinner with you," Danny said. "When you get better."

Danny saw a flicker of a smile cross Mack's face. Outside the car, two orderlies rushed out with a stretcher.

Behind them were two nurses.

One of them was Ma.

CHAPTER 12

The next twenty-four hours rushed by in a blur of sirens and blood and moaning, shouting men. But Danny barely had time to think about any of it. He was too busy.

After that first moment when he and Ma saw each other — Ma hugged Danny so tight she almost cracked his ribs, and he hugged her back even tighter — she put Danny to work in the hospital. Hundreds of Hickam men had been wounded. They were the lucky ones. Dozens had died when a bomb destroyed the barracks while men were just waking up. Dozens more never made it out of the dining hall when a bomb set it on fire. Others had been hit on runways, in hangars, or while firing machine guns at the bombers.

There were only two doctors and two nurses at Hickam. They needed every spare hand they could find.

Danny helped soldiers and volunteers make beds and sweep glass off the floor. He rolled bandages and found extra blankets for men recovering from surgery. He watched Ma as she hurried from man to man, changing bandages, holding hands, never flinching. Mrs. Sudo was right — she was brave. A few times Danny managed to peep in on Mack. Ma said he'd been given a powerful drug to take away the pain. He'd lost almost half of his blood. But Ma said he'd survive.

As bad as things were at Hickam, Danny

knew they were even worse out on the harbor. All night reports trickled in: The battleship *Arizona* was gone, along with more than a thousand men. The *Oklahoma* was capsized, and more than a hundred men were still trapped inside. The *California* was sinking. The destroyers *Shaw* and *Cassin* had exploded. Other ships were badly damaged. For most of the day, Pearl Harbor was a sea of fire. Even men who managed to escape the burning ships had little chance of survival. Hundreds of planes at different bases had been destroyed or badly damaged. Hospitals all over Oahu were overflowing with wounded men. Danny heard that his school had been turned into a hospital.

Everyone expected another attack. There were whispers about a Japanese invasion of Hawaii. Danny tried not to think about this, about how easy it would be for the Japanese to take over the island with so many ships and planes wrecked.

The hours ticked by with no more Japanese planes.

But America was now at war. Danny knew it would be months or even years before the sound of a plane in the sky didn't make him jump.

It wasn't until the next morning that Ma and Danny finally got to sit together. Ma slumped in her chair, more tired than Danny had ever seen her. Her white uniform was spattered with blood. But she listened closely as Danny told her the story of how he had been with Aki when he saw the first planes.

Ma told him about the terrifying first minutes when the bombs started dropping on Hickam.

"We'll remember this moment for the rest of our lives," Ma said.

Then she let out a strange sigh. "To think, I got you out of New York because I wanted you in a safe place."

She shook her head, and Danny could see she was fighting back tears.

"I'm glad we're here."

The words came out before Danny realized what he was saying. And Ma liked hearing them. She smiled a little.

Just then, one of the doctors peeked his head in and said he needed Ma for surgery.

"See you soon," she said to Danny as she headed out the door. "Don't go away, okay?"

She was joking, Danny knew. Because where could he go from here?

But he thought with shame of his plan to leave on the *Carmella*.

Would he really have gone?

If those planes hadn't attacked today, would Danny be on that ship?

He couldn't say.

It seemed impossible that only twenty-four hours had passed since he first saw those planes. Because everything seemed completely different now. Not just the harbor, now in ruins. Not just America, now at war.

But Danny too.

Maybe yesterday morning he had been the kind of boy who would leave his ma. He would never know for sure.

But he knew this: He wasn't that kind of boy anymore.

CHAPTER 13

DECEMBER 9, 1941
9:00 A.M.

It was two long days before Ma and Danny left
Hickam.

The first thing Danny did was change his
clothes. The next thing he did was sprint up to
the Sudos' house.

Aki ran to him.

Danny had brought him a present—one of the airmen had given Danny his wings.

Danny clipped the gold pin onto Aki's shirt.

"Mama!" Aki shrieked. "Look!"

Mrs. Sudo stepped away from her clothesline.

She smiled at Danny and hugged him.

But Danny noticed her red and swollen eyes.

A feeling of dread came over Danny.

He saw no sign of Mr. Sudo.

Mrs. Sudo had Danny sit down at the little table where they'd had lunch just a few days ago. She sent Aki into the house to get his toy trains.

And she told Danny what had happened. Somehow, Mr. Sudo had made it home from fishing the night after the attack. But the next day, the police had come to the house.

They were searching the houses of all Japanese people in Hawaii.

Mrs. Sudo looked down. "They are looking for spies."

"Spies?" Danny asked.

"They said that local Japanese here had helped with the attack. They asked if they could search our home, and of course we said yes. Because there is nothing here we have to hide."

Mrs. Sudo pushed her lips together and took a ragged breath.

"But they did find something. Something they said proved that Aki's father was helping the Japanese. The sketchbook. With all of his drawings of ships and planes. They took it. And then they took my husband to jail."

Danny tried to understand what Mrs. Sudo was saying.

"What's wrong with drawing the ships and planes?" Danny said.

"They said he had given information to the Japanese about what ships were in the harbor, and what kind of planes we had. They said he helped them plan the attack."

"But didn't you tell them that's not true?"

"Of course we did, Danny. My husband has lived in Hawaii his whole life. He loves America. This attack enraged him. That night he came home from fishing, he said he wanted to join the navy — the U.S. Navy — and fight the people who did this to our beautiful Hawaii."

"Did you tell them that?"

"Of course," Mrs. Sudo said. "But they didn't listen. I heard they have arrested other Japanese people. There is a rumor that they are going to put all Japanese people in America in jail."

Danny couldn't believe that was true. Mrs. Mills always said America was the land of the free.

Just then, Aki came running out with his toy train.

"Danny play!" he said.

Mrs. Sudo patted Danny's hand and got up to finish the laundry. Probably the best thing he could do for Mrs. Sudo was to keep Aki busy.

And so he brought Aki back to his house and they spent the afternoon playing.

All that afternoon Danny thought about Mr. Sudo.

Was there any way he could help?

Nothing came to him.

Until later that night, when he was lying in bed.

Danny realized that there was one person who might be able to do something.

And the next morning, he went to the post office and sent a telegram to Earl Gasky.

There was no way of knowing whether Earl had anything to do with Mr. Sudo's release from jail a week later.

But Danny knew that Mr. Sudo was back, because he heard a shriek from the hill.

"Papa!"

An hour later, Aki had dragged Mr. Sudo down to meet Danny.

Of course Danny didn't mention to Mr. Sudo that he'd asked a gangster to help free him from prison. Who knew if the telegram had ever reached Earl. And if it had, who knew if Earl had even cared.

But right now there wasn't much Danny could believe in. So he decided to believe in Earl.

CHAPTER 14

DECEMBER 25, 1941
7:30 A.M.

On Christmas morning, Danny was awakened
by a strange noise.

He sat up in bed, wide awake, wondering if
he needed to wake up Ma, if they had to rush
to the air-raid shelter down the road. There had
been drills all week. Everyone knew where they
were supposed to go if the Japanese attacked.

Danny peeked around the blackout curtains on his window. Every house had to have these curtains. It had to be pitch dark at night so that the Japanese wouldn't see any targets from the sky. Danny hated being inside the sealed-up house. It made him think of being in a coffin, buried alive. It scared Danny.

Pretty much everything scared Danny.

You'd have to crazy not to be scared, with what was happening in the world, with America at war with both Japan and Germany now. More troops were arriving every day at Pearl Harbor. Soon they'd all be sent to fight the Japanese in the Pacific, even Mack, who was almost well enough to start running bombing missions in his B-17. Danny knew Mack was sad to be leaving; he and Ma were good friends now. Danny never did have to make Ma go out to dinner with him. She asked him herself.

Danny was scared for Ma when she went to

take care of the men at Hickam. He was scared for Mr. Sudo, that he might get arrested again. He was scared that something bad could happen to Aki.

But, Danny decided, being scared was better than being numb.

If he were numb, he wouldn't be able to feel happy, and there were times when he caught himself smiling. Like when Mack came for dinner, or when Mr. Sudo was teaching him to draw, or when Aki rushed by with his crazy monkey smile, with no idea that so many bad things were happening.

And of course there was Finn.

Finn was better now. Danny found out because Ma had been allowed to use the phone at the hospital to call Mrs. Mills. Ma wanted her to spread the word in the neighborhood that she and Danny were safe. Mrs. Mills told her that Earl and all of his guys had enlisted in the army. And the most important news: Finn was out of the hospital, and he was staying with Mrs. Mills.

Danny liked the sound of that. He was writing Finn a long letter about what had happened to him during the attack. Ma said that all letters from Hawaii would be censored; soldiers would read his letter and cross out any information that could help the enemy. Danny didn't mind. He'd even asked Mr. Sudo to draw a picture of Aki for him to send. Mr. Sudo said that instead he would help Danny draw the picture. It was almost done. It wasn't good. But it didn't stink too bad.

Danny put his head back down on the pillow. At least the morning birds had come back. He liked to listen to them sing.

But then there was that strange sound again, the sound that had woken him up.

It sounded like a baby whimpering. Was Aki out there? He hadn't wandered since his father came home. But Danny wanted to make sure.

He threw on some clothes and went outside to the yard.

He followed the sound to one of the prickly bushes.

It wasn't Aki.

There, shaking like a leaf, was that baby wild boar, with the one white ear.

Danny looked around. Its mother monster was nowhere to be seen.

The baby was alone.

Danny picked it up.

The baby had changed in the past three weeks, like everything else.

Danny held it up and looked the little guy in the eye.

He looked scared. And tough. And like he'd be happy to have someone keep an eye on him.

Danny wasn't sure if it was possible to keep a wild boar as a pet. In fact, he was pretty sure it was a very bad idea.

But at that moment, Danny decided not to think about it—or anything else—as he headed up the hill to the Sudos' with the baby resting happily in his arms.

All he was thinking about was how Aki would smile when he saw his Christmas present.

PEARL HARBOR: A MAN-MADE DISASTER

Like all of the *I Survived* books, this book is a work of historical fiction. All of the main events and places are real. All of the characters come from my imagination.

But the tragic events of Pearl Harbor weren't caused by an iceberg or a storm or a hungry shark. The attack on Pearl Harbor was committed by men who plotted for months to cause as much destruction as possible. Why did Japan's leaders do this? What happened in the months and years after the attack? These are complicated questions, and I couldn't answer all of them in the story. So here is some more information, and suggestions for how you can explore this event further on your own.

Lauren Tarshis

Why did the Japanese attack Pearl Harbor?

Today, the country of Japan is one of America's closest friends in the world. But in the 1930s, the relationship between the two countries was tense. Japan is a small country with few natural resources. At the time, Japan's leaders wanted more wealth and power. To achieve this, Japan's leaders began taking over lands that belonged to its neighboring countries, including China. Their plan was to build an empire, a collection of countries that Japan would control completely.

Japan's military leaders knew there was only one country on earth with the firepower to stop them: America. By bombing our ships and planes at Pearl Harbor, the Japanese believed they would — in a matter of hours — eliminate America as a threat.

How did America respond to the attacks?

The United States' first reaction was total shock. Few people ever imagined that Japan could seriously threaten America. Experts had under-estimated the skill of the Japanese military and the sophistication of their planes. In the first minutes of the attack, many people, even top military officers at Pearl Harbor, refused to believe that it was Japan dropping the bombs. Shock turned to horror, fear, and sadness. But then, very quickly, Americans became united and fiercely determined. The next day, Franklin D. Roosevelt appeared before our Congress and made a speech that is still one of the most famous in American history. He said that the date December 7th, 1941, would "live in infamy," meaning it would always be remembered as a day a great evil was committed. Thirty minutes later, America declared war on Japan. Millions of Americans rushed to join the military.

Our enemy was not only Japan, but Germany too. Those countries had made a secret agreement to fight together. America joined forces with England and France, which had been fighting against Germany since 1939. Our partnership with England and France, which eventually included Russia as well, became known as the "Allied forces." Japan joined Germany and Italy. Together they were known as the "Axis powers."

This fight became what we now call World War II. Between 1939 and 1945, the war raged throughout Europe and many small islands in the Pacific. It would become the bloodiest war in history; nearly 60 million people died, including more than 400,000 American soldiers. (In my imagination, Mack makes it back from his B-17 bombing runs alive to marry Danny's mom.)

After years of brutal fighting, America and the Allied forces finally won the war.

After the bombing of Pearl Harbor, what happened to Japanese people living in America?

In the hours after Pearl Harbor was attacked, the country of Japan became our bitter enemy. Many feared that the Japanese were planning to invade not only Hawaii, but also the West Coast of America. It was a frightening time in America, and for Japanese people living here, there were uniquely terrible challenges. Just four months after the Pearl Harbor attack, American leaders decided that Japanese people living in certain parts of the U.S. should be forced to live in special guarded camps far away from American cities. Entire families had to pack up, leave their homes and businesses, and move to these "internment camps." Approximately 100,000 people of Japanese descent, the majority of them American citizens, were forced to live in these guarded camps until the war ended in 1945. Today, the "internment" of loyal Japanese Americans is considered a shameful act in American history. The federal government officially apologized in 1983.

What is Pearl Harbor today?

Today, Pearl Harbor is still a major military base. It is also a monument and graveyard. If you go to Pearl Harbor, you can visit the USS *Arizona* Memorial. This is the final resting place for many of the sailors and marines who died when the ship exploded. It is also a beautiful monument where you can explore what happened that day.

The memorial is built over the sunken battleship, which rests in 40 feet of water at the bottom of the harbor. The ship still leaks drops of oil that rise to the surface of the water. I was lucky enough to visit this memorial. The drops of oil made me think of the tears that are still shed over the lives lost in the Pearl Harbor attack, and the sorrows of the long war that followed.

DEDICATED
TO THE ETERNAL MEMORY
OF OUR GALLANT SHIPMATES
IN THE USS ARIZONA
WHO GAVE THEIR LIVES IN ACTION
7 DECEMBER 1941

"FROM TODAY ON THE USS ARIZONA
WILL AGAIN FLY OUR COUNTRY'S FLAG
JUST AS PROUDLY AS SHE DID ON THE
MORNING OF 7 DECEMBER 1941.
I AM SURE THE ARIZONA'S CREW WILL
KNOW AND APPRECIATE WHAT WE ARE
DOING" ADMIRAL A.W. RADFORD, USN
7 MARCH 1950

MAY GOD MAKE HIS FACE
TO SHINE UPON THEM
AND GRANT THEM PEACE

PEARL HARBOR TIME LINE

What happened on the morning of December 7, 1941?

3:40 A.M. A U.S. ship called the *Condor* is patrolling the waters just two miles away from the entrance to Pearl Harbor. Members of the crew spot something in the water. They believe it is a small submarine, but they aren't sure. In fact, it is a Japanese "midget" submarine, one of five sent in advance of the attack. The *Condor* reports this to a nearby destroyer, the *Ward*.

6:10 A.M. In waters 235 miles north of Hawaii, Japanese planes take off from six aircraft carriers. The first wave of planes includes 181 fighters, bombers, and torpedo planes.

7:02 A.M. From a radar post not far from Pearl Harbor, a radar operator sees an alarming cluster of lights on his screen. At least 50 planes are heading from the north directly toward Hawaii. He shows the officer in charge, a man with little radar experience. He mistakenly believes the lights on the radar screen are U.S. B-17 bombers returning to their base from California.

7:15 A.M. The crew of the *Ward* finally spots the submarine. They fire "depth charge" explosives and sink the sub. The crew of the *Ward* reports this incident to Naval Headquarters in Pearl Harbor, telling about the

sub. When Admiral Husband Kimmel
reads the message, he believes it
might be a false alarm and decides
to wait before taking action.

7:49 A.M. The first wave of Japanese
planes approaches Pearl Harbor.
The commander of the attack, Mitsuo
Fuchida, looks down on the quiet
morning and realizes that the Japanese
have achieved total surprise.

7:55 A.M. The attack begins as bombers
and torpedoes aim first for the seven
battleships. The *West Virginia* and
the *California* are hit and sink right
away, killing more than 200 men. The
Utah is hit and capsizes. The *Oklahoma*
is hit and rolls over, trapping
dozens of men; 32 will be rescued
after an agonizing 36-hour ordeal.

8:10 A.M. A powerful bomb explodes
through the deck of the *Arizona*,
igniting more than one million pounds
of gunpowder. The massive explosion
destroys the ship and instantly
kills 1,177 sailors and marines.

8:54 A.M. The second wave of 170
Japanese bombers arrives. This
time, they are met with anti-
aircraft fire. Bombs and torpedoes
hit ships throughout the harbor,
as well as planes and buildings
at the surrounding airfields.

10:00 A.M. The attack ends and
Japanese planes head back to their
aircraft carriers. The pilots
celebrate. The attack was a huge
success, but it was not complete. All
but three of the ships damaged in

the attack were eventually repaired and sent back out to sea. America's three Pacific aircraft carriers were, by luck, not in the harbor that day and escaped the attack completely.

MORE PEARL HARBOR FACTS:

- Number of American military personnel killed: 2,388

- Number of American civilians killed: 48

- Number of Japanese military personnel killed: 64

- Number of ships sunk or beached: 12

- Number of ships damaged: 9

- Number of American aircraft destroyed: 164

TO FIND OUT MORE
ON YOUR OWN:

Here are some excellent books for kids I discovered during my research:

Remember Pearl Harbor, by Thomas B. Allen (National Geographic Books)
    American and Japanese survivors tell their stories with great maps, charts, and timelines.

Attack on Pearl Harbor: The True Story of the Day America Entered World War II, by Shelley Tanaka, illustrated by David Craig (Madison Press Books)
    The author shows how the attack affected three different people: a boy living in Hawaii, a sailor on the USS *Oklahoma*, and a Japanese pilot. There are also plenty of great pictures and other info.

Pearl Harbor Child, by Dorinda Makanaonalani Nicholson (Woodson House)

The author was a girl living in Pearl City when the attack happened.

The Children of Battleship Row: Pearl Harbor 1940–1941, by Joan Zuber Earl (RDR Books)

Joan's father was an admiral, and at the time of the attack her family lived on a little island right smack in the middle of the harbor. Her story makes you feel like you are there.

The National Geographic Society has a great Pearl Harbor website, with an amazing "attack map" and a time line that shows the attack minute by minute: **www.nationalgeographic. com/pearlharbor**.

I SURVIVED

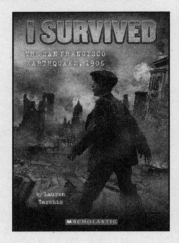

THE SAN FRANCISCO EARTHQUAKE, 1906

A CITY ON THE RISE — SUDDENLY FALLS.

Leo loves being a newsboy in San Francisco — he needs the money, but the job also gives him the freedom to explore the amazing, hilly city as it grows with the new century. Horse-drawn carriages share the streets with shiny automobiles, businesses and families move in every day from everywhere, and anything seems possible.

But early one spring morning, everything changes. Leo's world is shaken — literally — and he finds himself stranded in the middle of San Francisco as it crumbles and burns to the ground. Can Leo survive this devastating disaster?

I SURVIVED

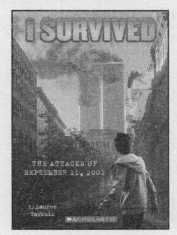

THE ATTACKS OF SEPTEMBER 11, 2001

A DAY THAT WILL CHANGE THE NATION...

The only thing Lucas loves more than football is his Uncle Benny, his dad's best friend at the fire department where they both work. Benny taught Lucas everything about football. So when Lucas's parents decide the sport is too dangerous and he needs to quit, Lucas *has* to talk to his biggest fan.

So the next morning, Lucas takes the train to the city instead of the bus to school. It's a bright, beautiful day in New York. But just as Lucas arrives at his uncle's firehouse, everything changes — and nothing will ever be the same again.

I SURVIVED

THE BATTLE OF GETTYSBURG, 1863

THE BLOODIEST BATTLE IN AMERICAN HISTORY IS UNDER WAY...

It's 1863, and Thomas and his little sister, Birdie, have fled the farm where they were born and raised as slaves. Following the North Star, looking for freedom, they soon cross paths with a Union soldier. Everything changes: Corporal Henry Green brings Thomas and Birdie back to his regiment, and suddenly it feels like they've found a new home. Best of all, they don't have to find their way north alone — they're marching with the army.

But then orders come through: The men are called to battle in Pennsylvania. Thomas has made it so far . . . but does he have what it takes to survive Gettysburg?

I SURVIVED

THE JAPANESE TSUNAMI, 2011

THE DISASTER FELT AROUND THE WORLD

Visiting his dad's hometown in Japan four months after his father's death would be hard enough for Ben. But one morning the pain turns to fear: First, a massive earthquake rocks the quiet coastal village, nearly toppling his uncle's house. Then the ocean waters rise and Ben and his family are swept away — and pulled apart — by a terrible tsunami.

Now Ben is alone, stranded in a strange country a million miles from home. Can he fight hard enough to survive one of the most epic disasters of all time?

I SURVIVED

THE NAZI INVASION, 1944

ONE OF THE DARKEST PERIODS IN HISTORY...

In a Jewish ghetto, Max Rosen and his sister, Zena, struggle to live after their father is taken away by the Nazis. With barely enough food to survive, the siblings make a daring escape from Nazi soldiers into the nearby forest.

Max and Zena are brought to a safe camp by Jewish resistance fighters. But soon, bombs are falling all around them. Can Max and Zena survive the fallout of the Nazi invasion?

I SURVIVED

THE DESTRUCTION OF POMPEII, AD 79

THE BEAST BENEATH THE MOUNTAIN IS RESTLESS...

No one in the bustling city of Pompeii worries when the ground trembles beneath their feet. The beast under the mountain Vesuvius, high above the city, wakes up angry sometimes — and always goes back to sleep.

But Marcus is afraid. He knows something is terribly wrong — and his father, who trusts science more than mythical beasts, agrees. When Vesuvius explodes into a cloud of fiery ash and rocks fall from the sky like rain, will they have time to escape — and survive the epic destruction of Pompeii?

I SURVIVED

THE GREAT CHICAGO FIRE, 1871

COULD AN ENTIRE CITY REALLY BURN TO THE GROUND?

Oscar Starling never wanted to come to Chicago. But then Oscar finds himself not just in the heart of the big city, but in the middle of a terrible fire! No one knows exactly how it began, but one thing is clear: Chicago is like a giant powder keg about to explode.

An army of firemen is trying to help, but this fire is a ferocious beast that wants to devour everything in its path, including Oscar! Will Oscar survive one of the most famous and devastating fires in history?

I SURVIVED

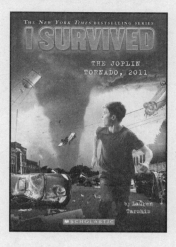

THE JOPLIN TORNADO, 2011

A DESTRUCTIVE FORCE IS ABOUT TO HIT THE CITY OF JOPLIN . . .

Eleven-year-old Dexter has always wanted to see a tornado. So when he gets the incredible opportunity to go storm chasing with the famous Dr. Norman Gage, he *has* to say yes! Dr. Gage is the host of *Tornado Mysteries*, the show that Dex and his older brother, Jeremy, watched every night until Jeremy joined the U.S. Navy SEALs and left Joplin.

Dex certainly knows how deadly tornadoes can be, but this one isn't heading toward Joplin, and wouldn't it be great to have a brave and exciting story of his own to tell Jeremy when he comes home? But when the tornado shifts direction, Dexter's bravery is about to get seriously tested . . .

I SURVIVED

THE HINDENBURG DISASTER, 1937

THE GREATEST FLYING MACHINE EVER BUILT IS ABOUT TO CRASH...

For eleven-year-old Hugo Ballard, flying on the *Hindenburg* is a dream come true. Hugo, his parents, and his four-year-old sister, Gertie, are making the thrilling four-thousand-mile journey across the Atlantic in a zeppelin as big as the *Titanic*.

But as the zeppelin gets ready to land, a blast rocks the *Hindenburg* and fire consumes the ship. The entire disaster lasts a mere thirty-two seconds, but in those few seconds, Hugo finds himself separated from his family and in a desperate race to escape the flames. The *Hindenburg* is doomed. And so, it seems, is Hugo. Will he survive this historic disaster?

I SURVIVED
TRUE STORIES

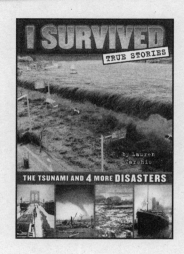

FIVE EPIC DISASTERS

REAL KIDS. REAL DISASTERS.

From the author of the *New York Times* bestselling I Survived series come five harrowing true stories of survival, featuring real kids in the midst of epic disasters.

From a group of students surviving the 9.0 earthquake that set off a historic tsunami in Japan, to a boy nearly frozen on the prairie in 1888, these unforgettable kids lived to tell tales of unimaginable destruction — and, against all odds, survival.

I SURVIVED
TRUE STORIES

NATURE
ATTACKS!

REAL KIDS. REAL DISASTERS.

The author of the *New York Times* bestselling I Survived series brings us more harrowing true stories of real kids up against terrible forces of nature. From the fourteen-year-old lone survivor of the shark attacks of 1916, to the nine-year-old who survived the Peshtigo Fire of 1871 (which took place on the same exact day as the Great Chicago Fire!), here are four unforgettable survivors who managed to beat the odds.

Go behind the scenes of the I SURVIVED series with Lauren Tarshis!

- Read Lauren's blog posts about her research and writing.

- See historical photos and learn facts about the I SURVIVED events.

- Chat with Lauren and other club members on the message boards.

www.scholastic.com/isurvived